Dear Reader

We always love revisiting towns we've created and enjoying a cuppa and a chat with secondary characters who have appeared in other books. Lewisville, a fictitious town set somewhere near Broken Hill in New South Wales, was no exception.

In this story we get to meet Brandon and, while he's not originally one of the main Goldmark brothers, he is every inch a Goldmark. Having fled his home town of Lewisville in order to recover from a broken heart, he returns home in time for his sister's wedding. And into town comes Clover Farraday—a woman who makes Brandon rethink and re-evaluate everything he's always known.

Clover finds that, like so many other women before her, she is not at all immune to the charms of those dashingly handsome Goldmark men, with their tall stature, their dark good looks and hypnotic blue eyes. Never has she met anyone like Brandon, and before she knows which way is up she realises she's fallen madly in love with him.

It was great fun to spend time with Viola, who is always baking and helping out her friends and neighbours, and also to see Geoffrey and his wife, Joan. We love all the characters—from Ned and May Finnegan to Marissa Mandocicelli. It's secondary characters like these that help bring to life the town of Lewisville, providing a colourful and romantic backdrop for Brandon and Clover to find their own happily-ever-after.

We hope you enjoy their story.

Warmest regards

Lucy

Lucy Clark is actually a husband-and-wife writing team. They enjoy taking holidays with their children, during which they discuss and develop new ideas for their books using the fantastic Australian scenery. They use their daily walks to talk over characterisation and fine details of the wonderful stories they produce, and are avid movie buffs. They live on the edge of a popular wine district in South Australia with their two children, and enjoy spending family time together at weekends.

A SOCIALITE'S CHRISTMAS WISH

BY
LUCY CLARK

MILLS & BOON®

First published in Great Britain 2012
by Mills & Boon, an imprint of Harlequin (UK) Limited.
Large Print edition 2013
Harlequin (UK) Limited, Eton House,
18-24 Paradise Road, Richmond, Surrey TW9 1SR

© Anne Clark & Peter Clark 2012

ISBN: 978 0 263 23097 0

Harlequin (UK) policy is to use papers that are natural, renewable and recyclable products and made from wood grown in sustainable forests. The logging and manufacturing process conform to the legal environmental regulations of the country of origin.

Printed and bound in Great Britain
by CPI Antony Rowe, Chippenham, Wiltshire

Recent titles by Lucy Clark:

FALLING FOR DR FEARLESS
DIAMOND RING FOR THE ICE QUEEN
THE BOSS SHE CAN'T RESIST
WEDDING ON THE BABY WARD
SPECIAL CARE BABY MIRACLE
DOCTOR DIAMOND IN THE ROUGH

**These books are also available in
eBook format from www.millsandboon.co.uk**

To Brandon & Clover—
congratulations on finding your happily-ever-after!
Ps 93:4

CHAPTER ONE

CLOVER FARRADAY turned up the volume on the car stereo and sang along with the song at the top of her lungs. Laughing, she couldn't remember when she'd ever felt this free. Being born into a privileged family, with a business mogul for a father, who was a constant source of media attention, and a caring, down-to-earth mother who had passed away when she'd been twelve years old, had left Clover feeling as though her life straddled two worlds. One was her father's world, where she spent so much energy and devotion trying to get his attention. The other was the world of medicine, which she adored.

Now, though, Clover felt free, vibrant, not bound by the rules of society or the gruelling expectations heaped upon her by both her father and her now ex-boyfriend, Xavier. Looking back on the past, she realised both he and her father had expected far more from her than she had been willing to give. Although she'd initially agreed to date Xavier, the one man who had been 'approved' by her father, Xavier's recent proposal for them to 'merge' both in business and in their personal lives had been too much.

'It's a sensible arrangement, Clover,' he'd said only last week. 'My company is merging with your father's. The deal is pure genius.'

'Deal?' Clover had looked at him as though he'd lost his marbles. She'd sighed. 'Look, Xavier, I don't have time to even think about any sort of… merger right now. I have a lot going on at work. I've just finished at the Blue Mountains maternity care centre and soon I'll be heading to Tathra for at least four months to help set up and train the staff of their new maternity care cent—' He hadn't listened, interrupting her only to make his point, one she hadn't been expected to contest.

'Once we're married, you won't be working, Clover. Your time will be filled with the social duties my late mother used to perform. It's expected that my wife will take over where she left off. Just think, you'll be patron of several very important and influential causes.'

'I'm not giving up my job, Xavier. Not for you. Not for my father. I don't care what's expected of me.'

Xavier had looked at her as though she were a recalcitrant child, then, taking a polishing cloth from his trouser pocket, had removed his glasses and given them a thorough cleaning, as though wanting to wipe away her words. 'I fear you're not yet ready to discuss this properly. Very well. We shall continue ever onwards and upwards for now.'

When he'd replaced his glasses, he'd smiled at her in that indulgent way she'd become used to, and asked if she'd wanted to order dessert.

Annoyed with his placatory and belittling attitude, Clover had declined the offer of dessert, excused herself from the table and made her own way back to the hotel where they had been staying in Port Douglas, trying to hold on to her temper.

After storming around her room for ten minutes, feeling completely stifled by the two men intent on controlling her life, she decided enough was enough. Packing her bag, she arranged her check-out and the hire of a car. She left a note for Xavier with the concierge, telling him she was taking some time out and would see him when she eventually returned to Sydney. There was no way she was going to let him ruin the rest of her much-needed two-week vacation with added pressure about what was essentially a marriage of convenience.

Instead, Clover found herself taking an impromptu driving holiday from Queensland's north coast, detouring through some Outback towns and then eventually making her way leisurely back to Sydney.

Everywhere she'd visited, complete strangers had welcomed her warmly and she'd enjoyed her time, making new friends and seeing the sights of the Outback, especially the amazing Uluru. As she continued to drive down the long, flat roads, the sinking of the sun making it cool enough for her to wind down a window, the music blaring out and fading away behind her, she couldn't remember feeling such a defining sense of freedom since before her mother had passed away.

Oh, how her mother would have loved this. To be free from oppression, free from rules and regulations, free from the expectations their upper-class living had imposed upon them.

A few minutes later, though, Clover was turning the music down and peering out the front windscreen, slowing the vehicle down.

'A road block? Out here?' She continued to decrease speed, astonished to note that the entire main road appeared to be blocked off. 'Where else am I supposed to go?' she asked, looking around the flat, barren landscape. She checked the car's GPS and realised that not too far ahead was a small town called Lewisville. She'd planned on stopping there for something to eat and to stretch her legs until the sun had set. She'd learned early on that driving just before dawn or dusk increased her chances of hitting wildlife that might be around the road—namely kangaroos.

As she neared the road-block signs, the houses of Lewisville in the background, she noticed a small tent pitched on the side of the road. As she brought the car to a complete halt, a man, dressed in denim jeans that had long ago forgotten any shape but his own and an old faded green T-shirt, which seemed almost sculpted to his firm torso, came out of the tent and walked towards her, a broad smile on his face.

'G'day!'

'Er…hello.' He was wearing a wide-brimmed hat, the kind she'd seen in television commercials when strong, strapping men were riding around on horses, cracking stock whips in the air above their heads. His sunglasses were the mirrored kind and as he bent down to talk to her through her open car window, she could see her own reflection in them.

Good heavens! Was that what her hair looked like? Self-consciously, Clover quickly brushed the wisps of dark brown hair which had escaped her ponytail back behind her ears.

'Sorry about the road being closed. Do you need to get through urgently?'

His tone was rich, deep and for some strange

reason was washing over her like a welcome, warm blanket on a freezing cold day.

'Er…' She closed her mouth and tried to get her thoughts together but all she could focus on was the well-muscled arm he was leaning on her car. When he lifted his sunglasses from his face she almost swallowed her tongue as deep blue eyes seemed to pierce her soul. Clover gulped, never before having been so instantly or incredibly attracted to a stranger in such a way.

She told herself he was just some Outback road-worker, who more than likely had women chasing after him, or, better yet, was comfortably married with a gaggle of children. As a child, she'd been taught how to speak to strangers, how to put them at ease, a skill she often called upon during birth deliveries when she was trying to get her patients to breathe and relax while she assisted their precious babies into the world.

He was still waiting for an answer and as her vocal cords didn't appear to be working, she did the only thing she could think of and shook her head.

'Excellent,' he announced, his smile beaming.

'Besides, it's probably better you're off the roads for a while, what with the roos and everything.'

'Yes,' she managed, quite proud of herself for producing a one-syllable word.

'So you'll be staying for the celebrations, then. Beauty, mate. I'm sure we'll be able to find a bed for you for the night but when there's a wedding in town, especially as tonight it's my little sister's wedding, there usually isn't a spare piece of floor space. Fear not, though, for Outback hospitality has never failed us yet. We'll get you sorted.'

'Uh…right.' She was having difficult processing his words but thought it easier to agree.

'Once you're through the barricade, keep on driving…' he straightened his arm out in front of him, the sleeve of the T-shirt pulling across his firm biceps '…going straight until you get to the hay bales. That's where you'll need to park because the wedding reception is set up in the middle of the street. Then just grab your stuff, walk past the pub and the medical clinic until you get to a house with a large sign that reads The Bride Lives Here across the front of the veranda, and you'll be sweet. Head on in, introduce yourself to Viola and she'll get you all sorted. OK?'

'Uh… O…K.' Clover's brain was still sluggishly trying to understand what he was saying. She wasn't sure whether it was due to the man's dazzling smile and good looks or if it was because there was a wedding being held in the middle of a town! 'Are you really sure it's OK for me to join in?' she asked, trying to clarify exactly what he was saying.

'Absolutely,' he agreed with a nod.

'Excellent.' She shrugged and smiled.

'I'll shift the barricade for you.' The man gave her a brief nod then strode purposefully towards the barricades and shifted them out of the way, waving his arm like a windmill for her to drive past. 'See ya later,' he called as she headed towards the town, continually peering in her rear-vision mirror as the handsome stranger disappeared from view.

Her attention, however, was quickly brought back into focus when a flash of blue caught her eye and a voice yelled out 'Hey! Watch it!'

It was only then she noticed two men, carrying

a large blue sound amplifier and hurrying to the side of the road so she wouldn't hit them, that she immediately slowed the car to an absolute crawl.

'I'm so sorry,' she called out the window.

'S'all right, love,' one of the men called back.

Clover decided to pay more attention to her surroundings rather than think about the easygoing man she'd met who—as far as she could see—had just invited her to his sister's wedding. She remembered what he'd said about where to park her car and when she reached the wall of high-stacked hay bales, she looked around for somewhere safe to park, but the only place appeared to be right in the centre of the road, as other cars, trucks and SUVs were parked around the area, forming an impromptu car park.

'When in Rome,' she muttered to herself as she switched the ignition off and looked about. Everywhere appeared to be a hive of activity, from people up ladders, hammering in nails and stringing decorative little lights here and there, to other people setting up tables and chairs. Some people were already dressed in their finest clothes, others were still in their work gear. As she climbed from the car, she could hear a band going through a sound check to make sure everything was in working order.

Clover glanced down the street where the two men who had been carrying the amplifier were now hooking cables and plugs into the back of the unit. She retrieved her suitcase from the boot and pulled it along behind her like an overgrown dog as she made her way down the street. When she passed the pub, which appeared to be over-flowing with people having a well-earned drink after all their hard work, she was astonished to receive a few appreciative whistles. She smiled shyly and gave a little wave to the men, who waved back vigorously.

As she continued down the street, people greeted her warmly, making her wonder if they weren't mistaking her for someone else. She went past the medical centre and even though there was a sign up indicating it was closed for the day, she couldn't help but stop and peer inside, interested to see what an Outback medical cen-tre might look like.

'Can I help you?' a male voice said from behind

her, and when Clover turned she found herself coming face to face with a police officer.

'Uh...yes. Sorry. I was looking for...' She closed her eyes for a moment, remembering what the handsome man at the road block had told her. 'Viola? Apparently there's a big sign out the front of the house.'

'Yep. Right this way.' The cop pointed to her suitcase. 'I'm Geoffrey, by the way. Are you just getting into town, eh? Cutting it fine. Would be a shame to miss it as the wedding's due to start in an hour or so.' Geoffrey walked alongside her as they continued down the street. 'So you must be from the Goldmark side of the family. Such a huge bunch they are but all of them are good value.'

Before Clover could correct him, he stopped outside an old weatherboard house with a wide veranda, ringed with a rail. The house looked as though it had been lovingly restored and seemed to stretch back quite a way, making it look small from the front but it was obviously bigger on the inside.

'Here we are! Just head on in. The rest of the

clan is inside.' As he spoke the words, there was the sound of a glass being smashed coming from inside the house. Geoffrey chuckled. 'I'll leave you to it.' He tipped his wide-brimmed hat, then turned and headed off back the way they'd come.

Feeling completely out of her depth and as though she were trespassing, Clover climbed the five stairs leading up to the veranda and tentatively knocked on the screen door. There was no answer.

'Hello?' she called, and wondered what she should do next.

'Hello,' a little voice returned and Clover peered through the screen door. 'Can you help me? I broke da glass.' The owner of the voice pushed open the screen door and Clover came face to face with a boy of about three years old, his lower lip quivering. 'It's a accident.'

'I'm sure it was,' she soothed, and, leaving her suitcase on the veranda, went inside to help out. There was a lot of noise coming from the other end of the house, children laughing and playing, women talking and someone asking everyone if they'd seen a pair of black patent shoes.

Clover followed the little boy into the kitchen, where she discovered a stool pushed up to an open cupboard and a glass smashed on the floor beneath the stool. 'It's a accident,' he said again, his lip still wobbling as he looked up at her with big blue eyes, blue eyes that were the exact colour as those of the handsome man she'd met at the road block. Perhaps this was his son? Clover swallowed over the disappointment that the man was already married with a family of his own and focused on the problem at hand.

'We need a dustpan and brush,' she told the little boy, who immediately turned and ran towards a tall cupboard beside the refrigerator.

'In here,' he said, and swung open the door with vigour. Within another minute Clover had the little boy sitting on the stool she'd moved to the other side of the kitchen to keep him safe and was sweeping up the broken glass.

'I see they've set you to work straight away,' a deep voice said from the doorway into the kitchen, and Clover looked up to find her handsome road-block man staring down at her.

'It's a accident, Uncle Brandon,' the little boy told him in earnest.

Uncle? Clover's interest was once more piqued. Brandon? She watched as he walked towards the boy. The name suited him.

'I'm sure it was, scallywag.' Brandon scooped the boy off the stool and swung him into his arms. 'What about using the tumblers Aunty Vi keeps nice and low for you, eh?' With the boy still in his arms, he located a green tumbler from a low cupboard then retrieved a jug of cold water from the fridge.

Clover stood, all the shards of glass swept into the dustpan. 'Where should I dispose of the evidence?'

Brandon chuckled, such a nice, warm sound that washed calmly over her, and set the thirsty three-year-old down, taking the dustpan from her. 'Leave it with me.' With that he winked at her and headed out the front door. Clover looked at the boy, who was drinking as though he'd just crawled through a desert. When he was finished, he stood on tiptoe and dropped the green tumbler into the sink then turned to look at her, no longer any sign of worried eyes or a wobbling lip.

'I'm Cameron. I'm free and a *half*,' he told her, holding up three fingers as proof. 'What's *your* name?'

'Excellent question,' his uncle said as he re-entered the kitchen.

'Er…' Clover looked from child to man. 'I'm Clover.' She held out her hand.

The man slid his hand into hers, all firm and warm. 'Brandon.'

Clover's eyes widened imperceptibly at the touch and she swallowed over her suddenly dry throat. Why on earth were her fingers tingling? Why was her arm getting warm? Why did one simple touch from this man…a man she didn't even know…make her body react in such a way? She'd come to Lewisville to get away from men, hadn't she? Brandon's hands were smooth, not at all calloused as she'd expected given he'd been in a utility tent on the side of the road when they'd first crossed paths.

He looked from her eyes down to their hands, held in a firm grip, neither of them adding any movement to the action but seemingly content to just touch. It was the oddest of sensations and one she'd never received from a mere introductory handshake before. When he met her gaze again, she smiled and quickly withdrew her hand.

'Shake my hand, too,' Cameron demanded, and Clover dutifully obeyed.

'Pleased to meet you, too, Cameron.' She straightened and looked at Brandon once more. 'Er…are you sure it's all right for me to intrude on what is so obviously a family occasion? I mean, weddings are usually very personal and—'

'Brandon! There you are, and about time.' A woman rushed into the kitchen wearing a lovely light purple dress with an apron over the top, her grey hair pulled back into a soft bun and a pair of fluffy pink slippers on her feet. 'I'm glad someone relieved you from your road-block duty because as the man giving the bride away, you need to go and get ready.' The woman turned and looked at Clover.

'Hello? Are you a friend of Brandon's?'

'Mum, this is Clover. She's passing through town and so I—'

'Invited her.' She nodded knowingly. 'I'll sort things out. Now go. Get cleaned up and changed. Honestly!'

Clover smiled at the way Brandon allowed himself to be bossed around by his mother. He grinned at Clover, shrugged his shoulders as though to say *Why bother arguing?* and headed out the kitchen. He stopped in the doorway and looked over his shoulder at Clover. 'Promise to save me a dance?'

Clover was a little surprised at the request but found herself nodding as his mother shooed him out of the kitchen. Then she turned to look at little Cameron, who was watching the adults with great interest. 'Off you go, Cam. Time for you to get dressed, too. Your mum's in the last room down the corridor.' With that, Cameron headed off and Clover found herself face to face with the woman who was obviously the matriarch of the family. Was she going to ask her to leave?

'Hi. I'm Viola,' the woman said, coming forward and extending her hand. 'We're all a bit crazy today.'

'Understandable. Listen, if I'm in the way, I can lea—'

'Nonsense. The more the merrier, right? Now, tell me, Clover, do you know anything about applying make-up?'

'Er...a bit, yes.' It was the last thing she'd expected to be asked and nodded as though to confirm it. What with all the balls and parties and functions she'd been forced to attend from a young age, having her hair and make-up attended to, she'd picked up a few things here and there. 'Excellent. Marissa, my friend, was going to do Ruby's make-up but burnt her hand earlier this morning.'

And before Clover knew what was happening, she was whisked away, being introduced not only to the bride but to a plethora of other women and children who all seemed to be a part of this big, crazy family. It was the type of family Clover had always yearned for when she'd been younger and now, seeing and being absorbed into the haphazardness of the Goldmark clan, that secret desire she'd pushed away so long ago came flooding back.

After that, time seemed to disappear as she not only fixed the bride's make-up but showed the other women how to highlight their naturally beautiful features.

'Oh, do you have something to wear?' Viola asked as an afterthought as they all started on final preparations. 'It doesn't matter if you don't. We're all very informal but it's nice to dress up once in a while.'

Clover did a quick mental inventory of her suitcase and nodded as most of the clothes she'd packed had been suitable for a five-star resort. 'I think I can find something.'

'Good. Just change in any room,' Viola called as she headed off in search of the person who was now calling her name.

Clover stood there for a moment, temporarily alone in a strange bedroom in a strange house in a strange town, yet she'd never felt so comfortable in her life.

CHAPTER TWO

'DON'T you scrub up nice?' Brandon remarked with deep appreciation a few hours later. The reception was in full swing, the bush band playing their hearts out, the bride and groom dancing close on the makeshift dance floor as though they were lost in their own private world. Clover was sitting quietly at a table near the back of the festivities, just watching and enjoying being a privileged interloper on such an incredible event. She was also giving her tired feet a rest, having been asked to dance almost every dance since the partying had begun!

Attending an Outback wedding had been the last thing on her mind when her impromptu adventure had begun. She also hadn't thought she'd find herself drawn to a man who was, to all intents and purposes, a complete stranger. Quite often as she'd danced, she'd found herself searching the crowd for Brandon, remembering she'd promised him a dance and not wanting the night to end until she'd followed through on it. Yet most times when she'd spotted him, he had been busy chatting or laughing or dancing with someone else. Clover had worked hard to ignore the thread of disappointment starting to curl around her heart at possibly not being able to dance with her handsome stranger after all.

But now here he was, lowering his tall six-foot-four-inch frame into the chair nearly opposite her. Clover tried to tell herself that her increased heartbeat was due to all the dancing rather than the nearness of the suit-clad Brandon. She'd thought he'd looked good in old denims and a tight-fitting T-shirt but seeing him in a black suit, white shirt and red bow tie as he'd walked his sister down the aisle, Clover had been hard pressed not to swallow her tongue.

Now, though, the picture he made was even more sensually disturbing as he shrugged out of his suit jacket and draped it over the back of the chair. Next he undid his bow tie and rolled up the sleeves of his white dress shirt. His hair, which had been neatly combed earlier on, was now tousled, making him look incredibly sexy... and dangerous.

'I could say the same of you,' Clover remarked, her voice a little husky as her gaze drank him in. She sat up a little straighter in her chair and tentatively touched her long brown hair to tuck a tendril behind her ear. It was a habit she had whenever she was nervous and as a child she'd often found herself in trouble for ruining the style that had taken the hairstylists hours to create.

Tonight, especially, given she'd had next to no time to get ready, she'd simply wound her hair back in a lose twist before securing it with a diamond-studded clip at the nape of her neck, little wispy tendrils curling around her ears.

'Do you often drive around the Outback with the latest fashions in your suitcase?' Brandon asked, unable to hide his intrigue with the woman before him. Her dress seemed to be a sort of black-and-silver colour, slim, fitted and yet incredibly flowing and feminine. It looked as though she'd been attended by a swathe of make-up artists and hairdressers yet his mother had told him that it had been Clover who had helped out with the bridal make-up, thereby saving the day.

'I don't often travel by car,' she replied, then bit her lip, wishing she hadn't said that. It would be best if the good folk of Lewisville had no idea of her true identity. The Sampson name was well-known throughout the world and usually when people discovered who her father was, they tended to treat her like a visiting celebrity. She didn't want that, especially with Brandon. She wanted to continue being treated as though she was just Clover, a woman passing through town.

'Really? So how *do* you usually travel?'

She shrugged and looked towards the happy newlyweds, dancing in each other's arms, oblivious to everyone else. 'I don't travel much,' she said, hoping that would put an end to the conversation.

They sat in silence for a moment, both of them watching as Hamilton, the groom, who she'd discovered was Brandon's distant cousin, held his new wife as close as possible, looking as though he had no intention of ever letting her go. Clover tried not to sigh wistfully as the need to have someone hold her in such a way, pulsed through her. She also realised she'd been rather brisk with Brandon just now and should probably apologise. She took a breath to do just that but Brandon spoke first.

'I was away when they fell in love.' He gestured to his sister and her new husband. 'Couldn't be happier, though. Ruby deserves so much happiness after everything she's been through.' He shifted a little in his seat to face her. 'She came to live with us when she was fifteen, after her parents died. My mother used to run a teen shelter—'

'Ah, yes. Viola did mention the teen shelter at one point. So Ruby came to town and stayed?' There was a wistful tone in Clover's voice. Through tragedy, Ruby had been fortunate enough to find happiness. It gave her hope. Perhaps one day *she* might find true happiness, too.

'She did, and now Hamilton is going to carry her away, overseas to Tarparnii, where they'll be helping out with an organisation called Pacific Medical Aid.'

'I've heard of them. They do good work.'

'I spent the first six months of this year working with them,' he added, and Clover's eyebrows hit her hairline. 'I only arrived back in town two, almost three weeks ago now.'

'You're a doctor, as well?'

Brandon regarded her with a hint of concern. 'Yes.'

'You're the doctor who runs the medical practice in town?'

Brandon smiled. 'Yes. Why, you're not feeling unwell, are you?'

She waved his words away. 'I'm fine. I didn't realise, that's all.'

The two of them sat there at the table, silence temporarily falling over them. Brandon couldn't help but be captivated by this woman. He had no idea where she'd come from, no idea where she was going, and yet for some strange reason he felt compelled to ask her to stay in town, which was utterly ridiculous.

Hadn't he learned anything as far as women were concerned? He'd jumped too fast into a relationship with Lynn and look how that had turned out. He had to slow down, to be more cautious, think things through, and yet the lovely Clover was absolutely tempting. What did it matter if he had a little flirtation with a complete stranger at his sister's wedding? Clover would stay the night, leave tomorrow and he'd never see her again, so why shouldn't he flirt and enjoy himself?

The silence stretched on as they watched several people take to the dance floor as the band played a faster-paced song. The bride and groom, however, continued to sway from side to side, oblivious to the beat or to anyone else. Clover sighed. Now, *that* was what true love was all about—dancing to your own tune.

'That's a big sigh,' Brandon remarked.

'I've had a big day and one I didn't anticipate would end with a wedding. I mean, with me attending a wedding…not that I'm…'

Brandon chuckled and the warm sound washed over her, bringing a shy smile to her lips. 'I know what you mean. I'm glad you stayed, though. Apart from the fact that it would have been nigh impossible to get your car past all of this…' he waved a hand at the paraphernalia presently blocking the main street of Lewisville '…I'm glad you decided to chance it and stay.'

'Well, thank you for inviting me.'

Silence fell across them once more but this time Clover was more highly aware of the handsome man beside her. His firm physique, his hypnotic, spicy scent and the way he seemed to move with such fluidity as he stood and walked around so he was soon beside her, holding out his hand. 'You did promise to save me a dance.'

Clover shrugged and shook her head. 'It's all right, Brandon. You don't have to feel obliged to entertain me.'

'I'm not. I'm entertaining myself—and you *did* promise. Don't disillusion me by going back on your word. I can't abide untruths. Besides the bride and my dear mother, you're clearly the most remarkable and stunningly beautiful woman here. Why *wouldn't* I want to dance with you?'

Clover swallowed over her suddenly dry throat. He thought she was beautiful? 'Oh.' She raised a hand to her chest, slightly overcome at his words. 'Well…er…' She smiled, nodded and placed her hand in his, unable to believe the slight tremble passing through her body at the contact. 'Thank you. I'd love to dance…with you.'

'Excellent.' With a wide smile he led the way towards the dance area, navigating their way around several chairs and tables. Once there and without a word he pulled Clover closer, resting one hand at her waist and holding her hand with his other. Her skin was soft, her scent was like wild flowers on a summery day, and Brandon found it difficult to ignore the strong pull of attraction he felt towards this woman who was only passing through his town.

Again, the logical side of his brain warned him to be careful. The other side—the non-logical one that had often led him astray in the past—suggested he throw caution to the wind. Clover would be back on the road, leaving Lewisville to continue with her adventures. Their paths weren't likely to cross again, so shouldn't he simply let go of his expectations and enjoy dancing with a beautiful woman at his surrogate sister's wedding?

He breathed in again, somehow knowing he'd never forget her delightful scent, or the way she felt in his arms. Perhaps it was the fact that they were two strangers, enjoying each other's company, that made this moment so different. Or perhaps it was the alluring way she moved her body in time to the music that was drawing him in. She was certainly an experienced dancer.

Even though it was dark, the street was lit with twinkle lights adorning every building, other small lights placed here and there making the entire area feel as though it had come from the pages of a fairytale book. The music changed and a more upbeat song blared from the amplifying speakers. Clover began to loosen up and soon she and Brandon were zigging and zagging and laughing as they threw themselves into the rhythm. When the song ended, she edged back ready to go and sit down again, a little surprised when Brandon kept a firm hold on her.

'We're on a roll. Let's dance again.'

She smiled and nodded, readily agreeing as that was what she wanted, too. For so long she'd always done as she was told, putting other people's needs before her own, but not this time. This time she wanted to keep on dancing with

Brandon and was pleased he wanted it, too. The next song was slower than the others and as they moved at a more sedate pace, Brandon leaned closer so they could talk.

'Thanks again for helping out with the make-up and getting Ruby ready. My little sister looks incredibly stunning this evening.'

'She's naturally very pretty but I was happy to be able to help out. It made me feel as though I had more of a right to be here rather than just some stranger passing through—which is exactly what I am,' she returned with a laugh, her words close to his ear.

She tried her best to ignore the natural, earthy scent mixed with a hint of hypnotic spice Brandon was wearing. How was it he smelled utterly alluring? How was it they seemed to be able to pre-empt each other's dance moves as though they'd been dancing together all their lives? It was an uncanny sensation, to be with someone she'd just met and yet feel like she'd known him for far longer than just a few hours.

'Are you a beautician?' he asked. Clover swallowed, knowing she'd never forget his enticing scent. Did the man have any idea just how he was making her feel? Probably not. He was no doubt used to having this effect over women he met and yet she couldn't picture him as a 'player', a man who went from one woman to the next without so much as an afterthought. 'Mum said you were very natural when you were doing everyone's make-up.'

'No.' She shook her head for emphasis. 'I'm not a beautician but it was nice of her to pass that information along.'

'So…not a beautician. Um…how about a dancer? You dance exceptionally well.'

She smiled and shook her head. 'Not a dancer but I've taken more than a few dance lessons in my time.' Mainly because it was required of all young teenage girls in her social circles to know how to ballroom dance. 'Care to take another guess?'

'Um…' He thought for a moment. 'Professional traveller?'

Clover laughed. 'Far from it.'

'Then I'm afraid I give up.'

'I'm a doctor. Obstetrician, actually.'

Brandon pulled back and looked into her eyes. 'Seriously?'

She smiled. 'I give you the truth and yet you don't completely believe me.' She shook her head, a teasing glint in her eyes. She'd never had this much fun with a man before. 'This isn't a great beginning, Brandon. I suppose to you I look more like a beautician than an OB/GYN?'

'No. I'm just surprised, that's all.' He shook his head as though bemused. 'You're a doctor.'

'Snap!'

'Brains as well as beauty. That's a lethal combination.'

'Thank you…I think.'

'Oh, that was definitely a compliment. So, are you travelling around the Outback delivering babies here and there?'

Clover shook her head. 'Nothing so organised or so exciting. I'm just a doctor on annual leave.'

'Where did you start this annual leave?'

'At my apartment.'

He chuckled. 'That's not what I meant and you know it. Did you seriously plan to drive around the Outback alone?'

'Actually, it was more of an impromptu trip,' she answered, thinking of how angry Xavier had made her.

'Which originated…where?'

'Uh…Port Douglas. I'm heading to Sydney.'

He whistled. 'That's a long way.'

'And I've enjoyed every moment of it.' She shrugged, not wanting to talk about her life, not wanting to spoil the glorious memories she was making with him. 'I have noticed, though, that there are quite a few women here tonight at various stages in their pregnancies. Where do they go to have their babies?'

'Trying to drum up business?'

'Not at all. Just…curious.'

'At the moment, they travel to Broken Hill.'

'That's about two hours from here, right?'

'Yes.'

'So they leave their families and go and sit in unfamiliar surroundings just waiting for labour to begin?'

'Something like that. It's not ideal but out here sacrifice and change are part of the equation. A few women opt to have home births, which either I or Ruby try to attend if we're able to get there in time, but the majority of women head to Broken Hill and wait it out.'

'And if they *do* have a home birth and require hospitalisation? What happens then?'

'Then we call in the emergency helicopter. Of course, there's also the Royal Flying Doctor Service.'

'Still, it must be so disjointing for the women.'

'It can be.' Brandon paused and angled his head to the side, considering her words. 'Why? Do you have some thoughts on the subject?'

Clover beamed brightly as they continued to move around the dance floor. 'And I thought you'd never ask!' With that, she told him about the maternity care centre she'd spent the better part of last year setting up. 'Women who live there can now choose between the hospital or the maternity centre. It's attended by trained specialists and not only gives them a place to deliver their babies but also provides much-needed support for those first few months postnatal. See, that's where this model of maternity care is different from all others.'

Brandon smiled, listening with great interest to what Clover was saying but also appreciating her passion. It was clear that setting up this centre had meant a great deal to her. He admired people who not only had a real passion for a cause but also followed through and did something about it, trying hard to make the lives of their patients that much easier.

A woman with passion—he could see it in her eyes as she spoke. Lynn hadn't really had a passion, not as far as other people went. She'd only cared about herself, about what she could get from others, that much had been crystal clear and as Brandon felt the anger of his ex-girlfriend's deception begin to return, he quickly shoved it aside, instead focusing on dancing and listening to his new friend Clover.

'So many women, especially first-time mothers, feel lonely and isolated and completely unsure of what to do with a newborn baby, and with this new working model, the maternity care centre is there to provide them with support and strategies to help them cope.'

'It sounds as though it would also help decrease

the effects of postnatal distress and depression for the mothers.'

'Well, that is one of the proposed outcomes. However, the clinic in the Blue Mountains hasn't been running long enough for us to have any conclusive data on the matter but there is a team in place monitoring it closely.'

'It sounds as though you'd like to be in the Blue Mountains, running the centre yourself.'

Clover sighed so heavily Brandon was a little surprised. 'It would be nice but due to its success a medical centre in Tathra, on the East coast, has also indicated its willingness to open one, which means I'm headed there to help set programmes in place and train the staff.'

'Sounds like an interesting job. And where to after Tathra?'

Clover shrugged. 'Not sure yet. Might just be back to the hospital.'

'When you're not setting up clinics, where do you usually work?'

'Small private hospital in Sydney—St. Aloysius.'

He raised an eyebrow. 'I've heard of it. Prestigious.'

'So some say.' She would say it was full of snobby specialists who overcharged for everything. Both her father and Xavier were on the board of directors of the hospital, which meant they'd managed to infiltrate almost every aspect of her life.

When she'd first told her father she wanted to study medicine, he'd given her a lecture about her duty as a Sampson and how being patron of different organisations was a better way to help people rather than literally cleaning up their messes. However, the next day a message had been passed on through her father's personal assistant, saying he'd approve her choice of career but only if she achieved top marks.

'No daughter of mine is going to just scrape through with average grades,' he'd reiterated when she'd thanked him for his approval. 'You're a Sampson, Clover. Never forget that.'

And so Clover had worked exceedingly hard during medical school in an effort to make her father proud, in an effort to garner attention from him, the same attention she'd been trying to gain since she'd been twelve years old and her mother had passed away.

The poor, bereft child had thought she'd be able to grieve with her father, that their combined loss might, in some small way, bridge the gap that had existed between them her whole life. It hadn't. Instead, she'd become another commodity for her father to manage and the only time he ever gave her real attention was when she achieved the goals they'd agreed upon.

He no doubt wouldn't be too proud that she'd rejected Xavier's ridiculous proposal and that she'd also taken off, daring to do her own thing for once in her life. She shook her head. She didn't want to think about her father and Xavier right now. She was at a wedding, dancing with a handsome stranger, but when she glanced up to look at Brandon she was astonished to find him watching her closely.

Dancing with a man, chatting easily with someone she found incredibly attractive, was something she'd never really been good at. Sure, she'd been taught how to make small talk, how to put people at ease, and she could do that...but not with someone she was attracted to.

It was one of the reasons why she'd agreed to date Xavier in the first place. He was nice, pleasant, safe and gave her a bit more of an opportunity to see her father. Now, with his ridiculous proposal, Xavier had changed all that and he most certainly did not set her heart racing with one simple look, the way Brandon was doing right now.

The song ended but neither Clover nor Brandon seemed to notice, both of them still moving around the dance floor, not caring that the band had once more picked up the tempo. 'I'm really liking the sound of this care centre,' Brandon remarked a moment later, breaking the strange and exciting awareness surrounding them. 'To have a centre like that here in Lewisville would certainly solve the immediate problem of women heading to Broken Hill for a few weeks but would also assist with postnatal care. There are so many women in the town, women who have already raised their families, who would be able to provide not only support but advice, as well.'

'Exactly.'

Brandon steered her towards an empty table, away from the loudness of the dance floor so they could talk more freely without having to shout…and without having to lean in close to direct their words into each other's ears. Whatever scent Clover was wearing was beginning to drive him to distraction and for a while there, as they'd danced, all he'd been able to focus on was the way she would angle her body closer to his, the way her luscious mouth moved, her eyes captivating his soul and…yes, it was time to get off the dance floor and put some much-needed distance between him and his beautiful stranger.

Besides, her clinic idea did sound perfect for Lewisville and as such he needed to concentrate more effectively.

He held the chair for her as she sat, then came to sit beside her, angling his chair so they were facing each other. 'I could apply for government funding, get a grant to set up a care centre here.' His thoughts continued to bubble. 'It could be set up in the empty house next door to my mother's place, as it's been vacant for the past two years.'

Excitement filled his tone and Clover found it infectious. She nodded encouragingly.

'I was thinking of expanding the clinic in town anyway as Ruby's going to begin studying again, wanting to specialise in paediatrics, and then after they return from Tarparnii there will be three of us in town available to provide care. And if you're happy to send me the information on the Blue Mountains clinic, it'll make applying for funding that much easier.'

'I'd be more than happy to do that for you.'

Brandon looked at her and slowly shook his head in bemusement. 'You're like an angel sent from above, Clover...' He stopped. 'I don't even know your last name.'

She shrugged. 'It's not important.' She didn't want to talk about anything to do with her life. Instead, she just wanted to live in this bubble world, this fairytale in the middle of the Outback. 'The important thing is to help these women.'

'Yes.' He was slightly curious why she didn't want to tell him her last name but brushed it aside. What did it matter? She'd be leaving in the morning after providing him with just the project he'd been searching for. He leaned forward and pressed a spontaneous kiss to her cheek.

Clover's eyes widened in surprise and she raised a hand to her cheek, covering the spot where his warm lips had left their delightful imprint. 'What did you do that for?' she asked, her words barely above a whisper, and she was surprised that given the music surrounding them he'd actually heard.

'To thank you.' He paused, intrigued by the way the simple action of touching his lips to her soft, smooth cheek had caused a fire to begin burning in his gut. 'Don't people in Sydney do that?'

Clover slowly shook her head. 'No. No, they don't.'

'Then I'm sorry if it made you feel uncomfortable.' Although he was having a difficult time reconciling the way he'd felt a sharp jolt of desire shoot through him the instant his lips had touched her skin. That had never happened to him before.

'Oh, no,' she quickly added, dropping her hand back into her lap. 'It didn't. You just…surprised me. A good surprise. I liked it. It's a nice way of saying thank you.' She was babbling now and closed her eyes for a moment in order to try and desperately gain control over her emotions, but the severe shock of tingles caused by Brandon's sweet kiss on her cheek was still affecting her equilibrium.

'Good.' His wide smile, one that made his blue eyes twinkle, did nothing at all to help her nerves settle down. 'So...' He shifted back in his chair and stretched his long legs out in front of him, leaning an elbow on the table and giving her his undivided attention. 'Tell me more about the care centre.'

Clover couldn't believe how incredibly comfortable she felt with Brandon. When she'd woken up that morning she hadn't even known of his existence and yet now she somehow felt as though she'd known him all her life. It was odd and relaxing and fantastic all at the same time.

The two of them chatted for quite a while, Clover excited to discuss her pet project with someone who was genuinely interested. They could have easily spent the rest of the night deep in conversation but were interrupted as the music came to a stop and the PA system squealed. Hamilton's oldest brother, Edward, who was the MC for the event, took to the microphone.

'All right, all you Jacks and Jillaroos, it's time for that ridiculous yet time-honoured tradition of the garter and bridal-bouquet toss.'

There was a combined cheer and groan but one stern look from Ruby made *everyone* cheer. This was her wedding and things were going to happen her way. Clover couldn't help but admire Brandon's surrogate sister. She sure had gumption. Both the bride and the groom stepped up to the microphone.

'We'll do the men first,' Ruby announced, Hamilton's arm firmly around her waist. Then she lifted her leg and put it on a chair. With the roar of the crowd, some good-natured ribbing and clapping, Hamilton lifted up the skirt on the bride's dress until he'd revealed her leg. A few of the men whistled but almost choked on their tongues when Hamilton glared them down for ogling his wife. It was all in good fun and soon he was twirling the garter around on his index finger.

'Who's going to be the next victim…er…lucky man to get hitched?' Hamilton asked as Ruby held the microphone to his mouth. 'Hey—Bart.' Hamilton laughed as he caught sight of his older, and only single, brother, trying to slink away into the distance. 'Get over there with the rest of the single blokes.' Hamilton looked around the crowd. 'You too, Brandon,' he called to his cousin.

'That's your cue,' Clover remarked sweetly, and couldn't help but smile as Brandon moaned.

'Do I have to?'

'Your sister seems quite insistent,' Clover added, giggling as he reluctantly rose to his feet. He'd taken only one step towards the crowd before he turned and held out his hand.

'I'll do the garter-toss thing only if you agree to do the bridal-bouquet thing.'

Clover leaned back in her chair, not at all sure that was a good idea. 'But I don't know anyone here. I'm an interloper.' She looked around and realised that quite a few people were watching them, Ruby now insisting into the microphone that the garter toss wasn't going to take place until Brandon took his rightful position amongst the crowd of single men.

'Brandon! Brandon!' a few of the other blokes began to chant, and even more people looked their way. Clover started to squirm uncomfortably in her chair but Brandon only stepped closer, holding his hand out to her and shaking his head a little.

'I'm not going until you agree, Clover. As a newcomer to the town, it's imperative you partake in all the silly traditions we uphold, no matter how outdated they might be by today's standards.'

She looked around, more people joining in the chant, more people watching the two of them. Then she looked into Brandon's eyes and saw that he was one hundred per cent serious. He wasn't going to move until she agreed.

'I'm happy to wait but I don't think the crowd will.' There was a teasing glint to his eyes mixed with a healthy dose of stubbornness.

'Oh…all right, then,' she said, and put her hand

in his, once more feeling the tingles of antici-pation flooding through her. 'You're certifiably nuts, Brandon Goldmark,' she muttered, but his answer was only to laugh and lead them into the cheering throng.

Clover watched from the sidelines as Brandon took his place with the other single men at this crazy Outback wedding. She'd been to plenty of weddings throughout her life, all of them run with the strictest decorum and pomp and ceremony, where no bride had ever tossed her bouquet, let alone the groom tossing a garter removed from his wife's leg!

She found herself laughing and clapping and cheering along with everyone else as a count-down began, the atmosphere completely infec-tious. Hamilton turned his back to the group and tossed the garter into the air and down, down, down it came. Some of the men jostled, pretend-ing it was a football heading their way and in their jostling, the white silky garter landed slap-bang in Brandon's hand.

'What? But I wasn't even trying!' he instantly

protested, but all he received in reply was loud raucous laughter and a round of applause.

'Hey, Vi,' Hamilton called. 'Looks like you'll be planning another wedding soon!'

'Fine by me,' Viola called back and then to Clover's surprise Viola's gaze rested on her. What was *that* supposed to mean? she wondered.

'And now for the ladies,' Ruby said, wanting to keep the festivities rolling. 'All right—all eligible women front and centre.'

'Your turn,' Brandon remarked as he sauntered towards her, twirling the garter around on his index finger. 'A deal's a deal, Clover.'

'Come on.' Ruby was encouraging.

'And I expect you to really put a bit of effort into it,' Brandon couldn't help but tease.

Clover levelled him with a look. 'I'll put as much effort into it as you did.' With a slight shake of her head and rolling her eyes, she headed into the middle of the dance floor with the other single women.

Ruby turned her back to the women and then on the count of three she tossed the beautiful bouquet of red, pink, purples and blue Outback wildflowers into the air.

Clover kept her eye on the bouquet the entire time and while the flowers seemed to be sailing in slow motion, and even though she didn't believe in this silly tradition whatsoever, she silently wished that perhaps one day she might find the right man for her. It was only after seeing Ruby and Hamilton, so desperately happy, uncaring what others thought of them as they danced to their own tune, that she'd realised just how much she *wanted* that level of happiness—true happiness.

The flowers twirled over once, twice, slowly descending towards the group of women. Hands went up in the air and Clover was astonished to find hers was one of them. In the next instant a cheer went up and she blinked hard, astonished at feeling the bouquet securely in her hand.

'I knew it would be you,' Viola said from beside her, and Clover turned to find Brandon's mother standing there.

'But…' Clover shook her head as she looked around at all the smiling faces, searching for that one particular person she needed to see, needed to witness his reaction, and when her gaze finally settled on Brandon, it was to find him looking at her in stunned amazement.

He'd caught the garter. She'd caught the bouquet.

'You're going to be perfect for each other,' Viola whispered, sighing with maternal pride.

'You and Brandon seemed to be very chatty last night,' Viola remarked as Clover sat at the large wooden family table, drinking a cup of coffee. She'd managed to get a few hours' sleep but knew if she wanted to make it back to Sydney by tonight so she could make her rostered shift tomorrow, she'd have to leave early. She'd managed to find a bed for the night at Viola's and had planned on packing and quietly leaving, putting a small thank-you card against the lovely vase that held Ruby's bridal bouquet.

Instead, she'd found Viola in the kitchen at five-thirty in the morning, fixing a bottle for a five-month-old baby. Clover had no idea which member of the large Goldmark clan the child belonged to but it didn't matter.

'We were discussing ideas for a new medical centre in town.'

'Yes, he mentioned you were a doctor. How fortuitous. Would you like to come and fill in for Ruby while she's overseas for six months? I'd certainly love to have you here.' Viola sighed and looked down at the baby in her arms, who was sucking greedily at the bottle. 'It's going to be so quiet when they all leave.'

Viola's words were soft and low, holding a hint of sadness. Clover wished she could come and fill in for Ruby.

'I'd love to stay but I'm rostered on call at the hospital tomorrow, then next week I leave for Tathra for at least the next four and a half months.'

Clover sighed and glanced out the windows. All the wedding paraphernalia had been packed up after the bride and groom had driven away in a Jaguar sports car just after midnight. Apparently, they'd been heading to a secluded cabin an hour's drive from Lewisville for a romantic evening. Once they'd left, everyone had pitched in, tidying the town and clearing the street so that by two o'clock the road was cleared and ready for use again.

She sipped her coffee and looked at Viola. 'It is beautiful here and I feel so…' she sighed, wondering how best to express the way Lewisville and its accepting people made her feel '…content.'

'Then you'll have to come back again. Even if it's just for a quick holiday. You're more than welcome to stay here any time and we'd love to see you again.'

'We?'

'Yes,' a male voice said from behind her, and she turned to see Brandon walking in the front door of his mother's house. 'We. I thought you might head off early and didn't want you to leave without getting a chance to say goodbye and to thank you once again for sharing your brilliance.'

Clover smiled brightly at his words. He thought she was brilliant? Beautiful *and* brilliant? No one had ever said those things to her before and a warm glow flowed through her at his praise. 'You're most welcome.'

She finished her coffee and stood, not wanting to notice the way that even in his casual attire of runners and tracksuit, his hair all tousled as though he'd just raked his hands through it rather than using a comb, he looked devastatingly handsome. After rinsing her cup at the kitchen sink, she walked back to the front door, where she realised Brandon was holding her suitcase.

'I'll put it in the car for you,' he ventured, and she quickly pressed the button on the car-key remote to unlock the boot.

'Thank you.' She watched him walk out the door and the sensor light came on, highlighting the firm muscles in his broad shoulders and back. She tried not to sigh at the sight and quickly turned her attention back to Viola, who was coming towards her, babe still in arms.

'Promise you'll come back?' she asked as she hugged Clover as close as possible without squashing the baby.

'I promise,' Clover replied, knowing in her heart it was true. Lewisville and its residents had somehow managed to infiltrate her defences and fix themselves firmly into her heart.

'And stay in touch. I'm an excellent email correspondent.'

Clover smiled. 'Will do. Thank you again for your hospitality.'

With a small nod Clover opened the door and stepped out onto the old veranda, watching as Brandon closed the boot of the car and walked towards her, shoving his hands into the pockets of his denim jeans. He wore another tight-fitting T-shirt, this one a pale blue, which only made the colour of his eyes more vibrantly hypnotic. What on earth was it about this man that she was attracted to? Instant attractions weren't a part of her well-ordered, well-structured world.

'Remember now,' he said, as he watched her walk down the steps towards the car, 'if you're ever in need of a change, just come on back to Lewisville and help me get this maternity care centre up and going.'

Clover smiled and nodded, knowing he wasn't serious. 'If I wasn't heading to Tathra, I might seriously consider it.' She looked up at him, unable to understand the way her handsome stranger had the ability to make her feel as though she really was the most important person in the world. Did Brandon Goldmark believe in instant attraction? Giving her head a little shake to clear it from her wayward thoughts, she headed around to the driver's side of her car and opened the door. Brandon followed.

'Anyway, it was great to meet you and I'll email you the specifics and protocols regarding the maternity centre as soon as I'm back in Sydney.'

'Sounds like a plan,' he agreed, as she climbed into the the car. Brandon closed the door and waited for her to put down her window. When she did, he leaned forward and smiled. 'I think this is where we came in.'

Clover returned his smile. 'I think you're right.' Desperately trying to ignore the tingles of awareness zooming around her body at his nearness, she almost jumped out of her skin when he reached into the car and tucked a stray strand of hair behind her ear.

'You take care, Clover.' His voice was deep, sweet, and held an intimacy that only fanned the flames of the fire already lit in her belly. He stared at her for such a long moment she wasn't sure what he was going to do next, which was why he took her completely by surprise when he leaned in closer and pressed a long and lingering kiss to her lips.

'Nice,' he murmured, drawing back a touch, unable to believe the tantalising and incredible sensations buzzing through him.

He'd wanted to kiss her last night but his logical side had won out, telling him he was once again moving too fast. Yet throughout the night he hadn't been able to think of anyone or anything else except his beautiful stranger. Kissing her, especially as he'd never see her again, had seemed the right thing to do.

The only problem he faced now was that he didn't think it possible to stop at just one kiss, his entire body urging him for more, and who was he to argue? Within the next moment he'd pressed his lips to hers once more, purely in the name of scientific research to see whether he'd have the same sensations the second time around. He did.

'Very nice,' he murmured.

'Yes,' Clover whispered in return, her entire body tingling with absolute delight. She'd just been kissed by a stranger and she had definitely liked it…probably far too much as she wanted him to repeat it again and again. With a sexy smile that melted her insides, he eased back, watching as she unconsciously licked her lips.

Her skin was glowing, her body was tingling, and now she was expected to drive? It took another split second for her to force her mind to focus on the task at hand and turned the key in the ignition. He moved away from the car and shoved his hands back into his pockets. As she reversed into the now quiet and sleepy town of Lewisville, Clover couldn't help but wonder at the sense of regret she felt in leaving.

Giving Brandon a final wave, she put the window up and set off down the long, straight, flat road—unable to stop glancing in her rear-vision mirror at the man who stood in the middle of the road, watching her leave.

CHAPTER THREE

Five months later...

WITH the car windows up, the air-conditioning pumping out cooled air at the highest setting, Clover slowed the car she'd purchased only yesterday as she came to the outskirts of Lewisville. She'd done it! The boot and the back seat of the car were packed with her clothes, books and photographs of her mother. She'd written a message to her father, letting him know she'd be out of town for the next few months, but no doubt it would be one of his personal assistants who would read it, note it and file it.

She'd contemplated letting Xavier know but had decided against it. On her return to Sydney after her impromptu trip from Port Douglas, she'd done her best to make him understand she wasn't going to marry him and she would never want to marry him.

'But your father has approved the match.' Xavier hadn't been able to compute what she was saying. Clover had shrugged.

'Then marry him instead.'

She knew it was rare for her father to actually give his blessing, especially to a man Clover dated. Back in medical school, Oswald Sampson had managed to successfully chase away—in his own unique way—boys she'd become serious about.

'Everyone has their price, Clover,' was all he'd remarked when she'd confronted him, asking him if he'd had anything to do with the sudden breakdown of a relationship. The first guy, Pierce, had been at medical school with her and one day, out of the blue, he'd broken it off, telling her they could never see each other again. After her 'chat' with her father, Clover had tracked Pierce down and asked him straight out whether her father had paid him off.

'It was a lot of money, Clover. Too good to pass up. I've got university loans to pay.'

In her last year of medical school, the same thing had happened, the one guy she'd become serious with had accepted her father's most generous offer and broken her heart. After that Clover had decided that enough was enough and refused to be a target for other men who wanted to make a quick buck simply by breaking her heart and discarding her like yesterday's leftovers. Why couldn't anyone like her...for her?

She guessed that was what she was hoping for by coming to work in Lewisville for the next three months. The last time she'd been here everyone had just accepted her as Clover—the woman who had been passing through and who had helped with a few hairstyles and a bit of make-up. Nothing more. Just Clover. It had been refreshing.

On her return from setting up the maternity care centre in Tathra, Clover had been astonished to find an email from Brandon waiting on her computer.

'I've advertised for an OB/GYN to come to Lewisville to set up and run the maternity centre. At this stage I only have initial funding for three months and have yet to receive any applicants for the position. I don't suppose you know anyone who would like to come to the Outback for three months…do you?'

Clover had quickly replied, telling Brandon she was back from Tathra, wasn't due to set up another clinic until March and, if he would have her, she would be delighted to apply for the position herself. Not only was she more than happy to lend her expertise to setting up the clinic but she was very intrigued to once again see the man who had been constantly in her thoughts, especially at night. She still wasn't sure why he'd kissed her and in some ways she wished he hadn't because the action had only made her want more.

It was one of the reasons she'd been eager to accept the job. Would the instant attraction she'd experienced last time with Brandon still be there? Had it been a fluke? A figment of her imagination? She hoped not. Seeing Brandon again, working alongside him, getting to know him much better were all valid reasons for her wanting to return to Lewisville. No man had ever affected her in such a way before and it definitely warranted further investigation.

Thankfully, Brandon had emailed her back almost immediately, accepting her offer of help. Viola had been ecstatic at the news and had declared that Clover *must* stay at her home for the duration of her stay. Clover had managed to take leave without pay from the hospital and then all that had been left to do was to pack everything up and drive here.

As Clover drove into Lewisville, smiling at the large red ribbons tied in bows around the trees and light poles in the town, she noticed a plethora of utes and other dusty vehicles parked near the Lewisville pub, the antennae and bullbars decorated with faded tinsel. Several houses, including the clinic down the street, seemed to be decked with twinkle lights, which would come on once the sun finally decided to disappear around nine o'clock in the evening. It was clear that Christmas had come to town and it only added to Clover's own excitement.

She still couldn't believe she was doing this— leaving Sydney to come to the middle of nowhere on the off chance that the man who had made her go weak at the knees with just one sensual look was interested in seeing her again.

After parking the car outside Viola's home, noticing that the house next door was busy being painted, Clover switched off the ignition and climbed from the car, delighted to stretch her tired body.

She was standing with the car door open, arms stretched up, head tipped back, sunglasses still in place, when he saw her. Brandon stopped in the middle of the road and stared. Clover! The woman who had caused him plenty of sleepless nights during the past few months was now standing three metres away from him. He blinked one long blink, as though needing to clear his vision, before he could accept that she was really back in Lewisville.

It had been desperation that had caused him to email her, wanting to ask if she knew of any colleagues who might be interested in setting up a maternity care centre in the Outback. Secretly he'd wanted her to accept the position but on the other hand he hadn't, preferring to let whatever had existed between the two of them at Ruby's wedding to remain in the past. He had no room or time for any sort of personal relationship.

Since Ruby had left first to go on her honeymoon and then to head over to Tarparnii with Hamilton to volunteer with Pacific Medical Aid, he'd been left holding the fort single-handed. Combine that with trying to set up the maternity care centre and he'd been rushed off his feet.

At night, he'd often dropped into his bed and fallen asleep instantly, waking in the morning with thoughts of Clover fresh in his mind and her name on his lips. It was odd. It was strange because he'd never experienced prolonged dreams about anyone before, not even Lynn. During his waking hours he was master of his own mind. While he slept, his subconscious appeared to have a completely different agenda.

Now, she was here. Back in Lewisville. Ready to help set up the maternity care centre, as well as give him a hand in the day-to-day general practice. He watched as she closed the door to her car and shifted her sunglasses to her head, before running up the front steps of his mother's house, where she'd be staying while she was in town.

He'd been on his way to check on the internal construction progress of the maternity centre, wanting it to look as completed as possible before Clover's arrival, but now that he'd seen her, he couldn't stop himself from heading towards his mother's house, delighted to hear the sound of female laughter as he bounded up the five steps towards the front door.

'Look who's back!' Viola announced to her son a moment later as he stepped inside the cool, air-conditioned house.

'So I see.' Brandon forced himself to keep his distance, not to cross the room and shake her hand, and he especially didn't want to embrace her in a friendly hug. Even being in the same room as her, that sweet, sensual perfume of summertime flowers she wore was already starting to wind its way around his senses. Why did the woman have to smell so good?

It was clear after thirty seconds in her presence that there was still a strong awareness between them. That was bad. At the wedding she'd been a ring-in, someone he'd thought he'd never see again and hence why he'd justified the way he'd behaved, especially when he'd given in to the urge to kiss her. Now, though, things were different. They were professional colleagues—and nothing more.

'Good to see you again, Brandon.' She wasn't at all sure how to play this meeting, feeling highly self-conscious beneath his gaze. Her heart was hammering wildly against her ribs and her knees felt as though they were about to buckle. She reached out a hand to the table for support. Ever since she'd left after Ruby's wedding, Clover hadn't been able to get this man out of her mind and now, standing in front of him, she realised he was far more handsome than she'd recalled. She liked the way his dark brown hair was all messed up, little bits sticking up here and there as though he'd been pushing his fingers through it in a haphazard manner. She liked his deep blue eyes and the way that with just one single glance at her body they'd managed to make her tremble all over. She especially liked his mouth. Her gaze dipped to his lips as she recalled with perfect clarity the way his mouth had felt on hers.

Brandon opened his mouth to say something then closed it again, the action causing Clover to raise her gaze back to meet his eyes, belatedly realising she'd been caught staring. She swallowed and quickly looked away, feeling highly self-conscious.

Although she'd initially accepted the position here, wanting to help with the maternity centre, she had also wanted an answer to the burning question that had been running around in her mind ever since she'd watched Brandon's reflection disappear in her rear-vision mirror last July. Had their time together been just a passing fancy or had there been something more to it?

After just a few minutes in his presence she had her answer—at least, from her point of view. Brandon might only see her as another colleague and nothing more.

Viola pulled out a chair at the dining-room table. 'Sit, sit and I'll get you a nice cool drink. You must be parched after such a long drive from Sydney. Brandon? Drink?'

'Yes, thanks, Mum.' And within the next instant he found himself alone with the woman
who, if at all possible, seemed to be more beautiful than when he'd last seen her. Today, as she'd
obviously been driving, her hair was plaited down
her back, swishing between her shoulders. She
wore flat shoes, denim shorts and a loose white
cotton top—comfortable driving attire.

'Do you mind if I don't sit? I've been sitting
for so long now, it's nice to stand and just stretch
out my muscles.'

Brandon shrugged a shoulder, remaining by
the front door and not moving towards the table.
She started to walk around the room, looking at
all the knick-knacks and photographs scattered
throughout his mother's open dining and lounge
room.

He swallowed, knowing he should probably say
something, but at the moment his mind didn't
seem to be cooperating too well. What was it
about this woman? Even her mere presence had
the ability to tongue-tie him. He watched the way
she moved, so full of grace, her movements fluid,
almost gliding.

'Er…no problem with the drive? Car went well?' he finally forced himself to ask after the silence between them seemed to stretch to breaking point. Where was his mother when they needed her?

'Yes, thanks. Everything went fine. No problems at all.' Clover picked up a snow globe of Mount Kosciuszko and gave it a little shake before replacing it. 'How about you? I hear you've been burning the candle at both ends, overseeing the renovations for the care centre and running your busy medical practice all by yourself.'

'Hear?'

She indicated the kitchen where Viola was still fixing drinks. 'Your mother's been emailing me, keeping me up to date on the Lewisville shenanigans.'

'Has she, now?' And why hadn't his mother mentioned to him that she'd been in contact with Clover during the past five months? He and Clover had exchanged a few emails when she'd first returned to Sydney but that had been purely professional when she'd forwarded the information about the care centre. After that he'd worked hard to put her out of his mind as best he could but the dreams had continued to happen and in the end he'd given up, deciding to accept the time he'd spent with Clover was nothing more than a fond memory.

Then, in the end, he'd had to contact her about the care centre, asking if she could recommend anyone to help. That had been the extent of their emails and really, the only personal information he'd learned from it had been Clover's surname—Farraday. Clover Farraday. The name suited her. He glanced down at his feet, trying to figure out what to do or say next because nothing made any sense at the moment. 'Well…' He jerked a thumb over his shoulder. 'I'd better head next door to check on the care centre.'

'Oh? Can I come, too?'

'Well…er…' Brandon didn't really want to be alone with her, not so soon and not when he was still trying to get control over his senses. 'The painters are in there today. How about tomorrow?'

'Oh, OK.' She'd nodded and forced a small smile but he could see the disappointment in her eyes. He remembered those big brown eyes all too well. He remembered how it would be very easy for a man to lose himself in them and now that he'd rejected her request, he felt instant remorse, wanting to change his mind and take her next door so she could admire all the work that had been done.

He realised he only wanted to do that so he could see her smile—properly smile, which obviously meant he needed to get out of his mother's house as fast as possible if he was going to have any chance of keeping his wits about him. Good heavens. The woman was more tantalising than his sluggish memory recalled. No wonder he'd had a difficult time keeping his lips off her.

With a nod, she turned and looked at a few of the wedding pictures hanging on the wall. There were several of the Goldmark men, Hamilton and his brothers as well as a few others. Clover pointed to one taken many decades ago. 'Is this your parents?'

'Yes.'

'Your father's very handsome.' Clover looked from the photo to Brandon. 'You look identical.'

Had she just implied he was handsome? Brandon blinked one long blink.

'Oh, my Bill was a wonderful man,' Viola remarked as she came towards Clover, carrying three long, cool drinks on a tray. 'Good looking but cheeky and fun loving.'

Clover smiled, delighted at the way Viola just opened up to her. Throughout her upbringing there had always been so many subjects that had been taboo and talking about the past, especially family, had been one of them. In the mansion where she'd been raised, there were no family photographs, no wedding pictures or memorabilia of times gone by. Instead, the walls were decorated with the latest in fashionable art chosen by an interior designer with, as far as Clover was concerned, horrible taste.

At Christmastime she'd never been allowed to help with any of the decorating. She'd never been able to string up some tinsel or hang an ornament on the tree. Everything had been organised by strangers. It was clear Viola was still in the process of putting her decorations up, a large box in the corner with brightly coloured tinsel spilling out of it. She wondered if she'd be allowed to help.

'He sounds wonderful.' There was a wistfulness in her tone, envying Brandon for being raised in such a loving and caring family. She looked from the photograph of a young and excited Viola to the woman beside her. The excitement was still evident in her eyes but the face now held years' worth of experience. 'You must miss him.' Her words were quiet, respectful, caring.

'Every day, my dear.' Viola looked at the photograph of her husband. 'But life is life and you cope with the hand you've been dealt in the best way you can so as to promote happiness, not only to yourself but to those around you.'

'Wise words.'

Brandon stepped forward and put his arm around his mother's shoulders. 'From a wise woman.' He kissed her head.

'Oh, get away with you.' She smiled up at her boy, then turned to face Clover. 'I've made up your room so it's all ready. Brandon, go and help Clover bring her things in from the car.'

'It's all right,' Clover replied, before Brandon

could move. 'I can cope. I know you have work to do and I wouldn't want to interfere.'

'Don't be silly. It won't take Brandon lo—'

'No, Viola,' Clover interrupted. 'I'm here to make Brandon's life easier, not more difficult or complex.' She waved both hands in a shooing motion towards the door. 'You go and take care of things at the maternity centre. Don't you worry about me.'

Brandon frowned for a moment before deciding it was best not to stand there and argue but instead to gulp down the drink his mother had made and get out of there as fast as possible. 'OK. I guess I'll see you around.'

'I guess you will.'

With that, Brandon turned on his heel and headed to the door, a frown of puzzlement furrowing his brow as he made his way down the stairs. Had his new temporary colleague, the woman who was only here for the next three months, just ordered him around? Had he just been dismissed?

Perhaps working alongside her was going to

be far more difficult than he'd initially realised, not only from a personal perspective but from a professional one as well!

CHAPTER FOUR

CLOVER sat on the porch swing later that evening after the sun had set, her legs tucked under her as she allowed herself to relax. A shower of rain had swept through the town at around seven o'clock, helping the temperature to drop a few degrees, but even now, at almost a quarter to ten, she could read on Viola's outdoor gauge that it was still twenty-seven degrees Celsius. The Christmas twinkle lights on the town buildings were all shining brightly, blending with the stars up above to make a magical sight.

'We're all up later of an evening, wanting to make the most of our summer light,' Viola had mentioned after the two of them had eaten and stacked the dishwasher. 'Early mornings, late nights and naps in the middle of the day when the sun is at its hottest. That's the way to do it.'

Clover had smiled, listening to what Viola had

to say but all the while glancing at the front door hoping that Brandon would stop by. When she'd tried to enquire innocently as to whether Brandon would be joining them for dinner, Viola had shrugged.

'We usually eat together a few times a week—probably more since Ruby left. He worries about me being alone but, honestly, on the evenings he's not here, I'm often spending time with Marissa or May or one of my other friends. I'm a busy woman,' she'd told Clover with a smile. 'And now I have you to keep me company, as well.'

When Brandon hadn't turned up for dinner, Clover had tried not to be disappointed. Perhaps that crazy awareness, that thrill of excitement, that powerful tug of attraction she'd felt at Ruby's wedding had been all one-sided. Perhaps after Brandon had kissed her goodbye, he hadn't thought about her since…or at least until he'd needed her help finding an OB/GYN for the clinic. Perhaps he saw her now as nothing more than a colleague and as such hadn't thought it necessary to drop by for dinner on her first evening in town.

When Viola had asked if she'd like to come across to Marissa's for a cup of late-night herbal tea, Clover had declined. 'I'm a little tired, what with the drive and all.'

'Of course you are, dear. How silly of me.' Viola had swiped a cloth over the now clean kitchen and picked up an old tattered book of recipes. 'OK, well I'll head off to see Marissa on my own. She's just developed a new recipe for shortbread cookies. Just sit yourself on the porch, pour yourself a cool drink and relax.' Viola had touched Clover's cheek with her free hand in such a comforting maternal way. 'Tomorrow's another day.'

Clover's eyes had widened at the words, tears beginning to gather. 'That's what my mother used to say.'

'Then she was a wise woman.' With a deep smile Viola had headed off to her friend's house situated not too far away. And so Clover sat on the porch swing, cool drink in hand, and absorbed the serenity of Lewisville. She tipped her head back, looking up at the plethora of stars and breathing in the fresh air, unable to believe how incredibly beautiful it was out here. Her mother would have loved it.

'Hi.'

At the rich, deep voice, Clover immediately sat up straighter, uncurling her legs and almost spilling the remaining contents of her glass.

'I didn't mean to startle you,' Brandon remarked as he walked up the steps and came to stand opposite her, leaning against the railing that ringed the porch. She'd changed her clothes and was now wearing a pair of three-quarter-length jeans and a comfortable T-shirt, her glorious long brown hair flowing freely down her back. He shoved his hands deeper into the pockets of his jeans, resisting the urge to touch it, to feel if it really was as silky as it looked.

'Brandon. What a nice surprise.' Her gaze instantly blended with his and she worked hard to ignore the increased pounding of her heart against her chest.

'Sorry I didn't make dinner,' he offered. 'I had planned to, given this was your first night in town, but I had an impromptu meeting with Geoffrey in the pub, where he needed to discuss the logistics for the up-and-coming billy-cart race.'

'Fair enough. Not that I was…you know… expecting you to be there. Of course you have things to attend to and…' She stopped, realising she was babbling, and quickly took a sip of her drink, hoping the cool liquid would help bring a bit of order to her jumbled thoughts. She was still perplexed about how Brandon could make her feel like an inexperienced schoolgirl by aiming one of his gorgeous smiles in her direction.

Neither of them spoke for a moment, the seconds ticking by and the atmosphere around them starting to thicken. Quickly, she cleared her throat and motioned to the town spread before them. 'I had no idea it would be so pretty here at Christmas,' she ventured. 'There are definitely more twinkle lights than at Ruby's wedding.'

He smiled at her comment and looked at the lights before them. 'It does look good, even though hanging the darn things takes for ever. Still, we're a town that really gets into the festive season.'

'You helped hang the lights?' Clover was astonished.

'Yes. Why wouldn't I?' Brandon was surprised at her question.

'I know plenty of medics who would think such a thing was beneath them.'

'Perhaps you haven't been hanging out with the right people.'

Clover smiled. 'I don't think I've done much... hanging out, as you call it, at all.'

'Why?' He turned and faced her directly. 'Are you a complete workaholic?'

'Maybe. I guess what I mean is I don't tend to socialise all that much.'

'And here I thought Lewisville wouldn't be able to compete with Sydney when it came to the social life.' He was watching her so intently, as though he was desperate to try and understand her. 'You didn't spend time with your colleagues?' He paused just for a moment, his tone deepening, his words softer, more intimately concerned. 'All work and no play isn't good for the soul, Clover.'

She tried not to squirm beneath his inquisitive

gaze, rising from the porch swing and walking to the other side of the rail, needing to put some distance between them. 'I prefer to keep to myself.' She shrugged. 'I guess…you could say I'm a very private person.' Especially when her father was clearly in the public eye. Well, that was fine for him but it wasn't the life she had chosen. 'I don't particularly like to talk about my past.'

Brandon nodded once, as though accepting her words, yet she could feel him still watching her. 'Didn't you have a happy childhood?'

'I had a…' She thought about the nursery in the mansion, about how she'd been provided with every new toy any little girl could desire. Clothes, electronic games, new phones, computers, books, cameras, anything and everything as her father decreed it. No child of Oswald Sampson would want for a single thing except perhaps the love of a father. 'Different childhood.'

Brandon wasn't quite sure what that meant but could see that if he pushed her for answers she would no doubt clam right up. Still, he wanted to know more about what made Clover tick and after his easy acceptance of Lynn when she'd first arrived in town and the way she had left him feeling bitter and hurt, his trust had been broken.

If he was going to work successfully with Clover over the next few months, surely he had a right to get to know her a little better—purely for professional reasons. He'd learned the hard way that where stunning, unknown females were concerned, especially when it was clear things simply didn't add up, he reserved the right to question, to dig beneath the surface and discover the truth. Perhaps he could push just a little bit more for tonight.

'A different childhood, eh? Did your parents divorce? That can always be difficult to deal with.'

'They didn't divorce, no. My mother passed away when I was twelve. My father and I aren't close. Anyway, I forgot to tell you, a pregnant woman called Lacey Millar stopped me in the street just before dinner, desperate for an update on the maternity centre because she really wants to have her baby delivered there.'

The words, both personal and professional, tumbled from her mouth and Brandon realised it was doubtful he'd get more than that from her tonight. He knew he needed to respect that but he couldn't help admitting that even those few words about her parents had only piqued his interest even further.

Discovering more about this alluring and enigmatic woman was definitely becoming a high priority, especially as the sensations he'd felt at the wedding hadn't seemed to have disappeared during the past five months. Seeing her today had only served as a reminder of just how incredible she'd felt in his arms, the way her scent had drugged his senses, the way her mouth had tasted so incredible when he'd given in to the urge to kiss her goodbye.

Brandon forced himself to look away from that delectable mouth of hers and kick-start his brain back into gear. What had she asked him? That's right. The maternity centre. 'Parker, one of the guys working on the project, told me the outside will be finished by tomorrow. There's still more work to be done here and there and a lot of the equipment hasn't arrived but we're getting there.'

'So will I be able to start running the courses straight away? I was talking to your mother about it at dinner tonight and she mentioned that she and Marissa Mandoc—' She paused, trying to recall Marissa's surname.

'Mandocicelli,' he supplied.

'Yes, thank you. Apparently the two of them are desperate to get the courses up and running. They're looking forward to teaching new mums-to-be how to practise putting nappies onto teddy bears and how to bath a large doll.'

Brandon saw the light come back into her brown eyes and couldn't believe how beautiful she looked. The lilt in her voice washed over him and he started to feel the stress in his trapezius muscle begin to ease. What was it about Clover that both relaxed and intrigued him?

'I do have a few queries, though,' she continued. 'Mainly pertaining to the delivery suites at the rear. Is it OK now if we go and take a look?'

Brandon shrugged and led the way, Clover following him down the steps to the house next door where he took out a set of keys, located the one he needed and unlocked the door. As they headed inside he flicked on the light switch, excited when the lights came on.

'I haven't been here at night since the renovations first began.'

'You've done an amazing job,' she said to Brandon. 'I know this used to be an old house but the decision to keep the front room as a lounge room was a stroke of brilliance. That way, when the women come in for sessions, they're nice and relaxed and comfortable and it really does promote the atmosphere that you're just popping over to a friend's place for a cup of tea or a chat about how to cope with sore nipples when breastfeeding.'

Brandon chuckled and Clover allowed the sound to wash over her. With the way he was smiling at her, it instantly brought back memories of the hours they'd spent together in July. Here was the man who had made her heartbeat increase, had made her knees weaken with just one look, who had pressed his mouth to hers in the most tantalising and promising kiss she'd ever had. He was the man who had filled both her dreams and her daydreams when she'd been in Tathra, setting up the other maternity centre.

He was the man who had influenced her decision to return to Lewisville, to see whether or not

the attraction had been a figment of her imagination. It wasn't and she couldn't help but wonder that if a simple, straightforward kiss they'd
shared had rocked her world that much, what
on earth was going to happen if she ever got the
chance to *really* kiss him?

'Anyway, from the schematics I've seen...' She
turned away from his alluring smile, knowing it
was best to focus on what she needed to talk to
him about. Professional. She had to be professional. He was her colleague now, not a stranger
inviting her to a wedding. 'I have a query regarding fitting the examination couch plus a humidi-
crib—when they arrive—and a crash cart into
the room.'

They headed down the corridor and studied
the delivery rooms at the rear of the centre. The
other seven rooms they passed were set aside
for those mothers who needed to stay overnight.
There was also a family room available for parents who might need to bring older children with
them. There would also be courses held for ex-
pectant fathers, teaching them not only how to

give a bottle and to bath the baby but also how to settle the baby in the middle of the night.

In the end, Clover suggested they shift the position of the examination bed and then everything should fit quite easily.

'We'll know more once all the rest of the equipment arrives,' Brandon said as they headed back to the reception area.

'Any idea when?'

'Still just after Christmas. That's the earliest we can get them.'

'Then we'll have to make do until then.' She stopped at the front desk and nodded. 'I really like what you've done here, that you've managed to adapt the schematics I provided you with for the needs of Lewisville.'

'It's a model to be proud of, Clover, and as its designer and creator you should definitely take credit for it. Naming rights. Proper recognition for everything you've done. It's a stroke of genius and garnering a lot of interest from my colleagues in other Outback towns.'

'Really?' She was completely surprised at this news. 'I just wanted to provide pregnant women who lived in remote areas with the means not only of delivering their babies as close to their homes as possible but also to provide a way for them to *learn* how to be mothers.' She looked down at her hands.

'I know my own mother struggled with it. She used to tell me how she was expected to know what to do, how to change a nappy, what to do if your baby had a fever, how to settle a child that simply wouldn't sleep.'

'You wouldn't sleep?'

'Apparently I was a very colicky baby.' Clover grinned then shrugged her shoulders. 'I remember her saying there should be more places where women could go to teach them *how* to be mothers, to have someone more experienced *show* them what to do.'

Her own mother had been provided with a nanny because no wife of Oswald Sampson should have to wipe a baby's bottom, but nine times out of ten Clover's mother had prided herself on looking after her daughter rather than handing on that responsibility. 'Mum wanted to *do* something but she wasn't sure exactly where to start.'

'Was she a medic, too?' Brandon couldn't resist asking the question and hoped that it didn't cause Clover to clam up again. The fact that she'd even mentioned her mother was wonderful and it was clear through the brightness in her tone that the two of them had been extremely close.

'No, but she would often tell me that I could do anything in the world if I set my mind to it. She'd also mentioned, on more than one occasion, that I was definitely smart enough to go to medical school and become a doctor.'

Clover shrugged and shook her head, realising she'd probably said too much but unable to stop herself. Brandon was very easy to talk to and that was another thing she hadn't experienced before—a man who actually *listened* to what she had to say.

'I guess she's had a bigger influence in my life than I've realised until now but she was always adamant about help for young mothers. There's still so much focus on the actual pregnancy and the delivery, and that's all well and good and still necessary, but what happens next? Keep them in hospital for a day or two and then send them home with a list of suggestions or a book that they feel they have to live up to!'

Brandon leaned against the doorjamb, attracted to the passion burning through the woman before him. Her eyes were alive, her words filled with power, her hands straight and often slicing through the air as she made her points. There was a healthy glow about her and even though he'd seen her dressed up all fancy-like at Ruby's wedding, there was no denying the beauty shining through her right now.

'A book only sets up ridiculous expectations, making the poor young mother feel as though she's failed, rather than catering to the individual needs of both mother and child. What's right for one child is not right for another. Every child is different and from my completed research, it was shown that even mothers with more than one child often had difficulty coping.

'*That's* what my hope for the maternity care centre is all about. Not just a closer place to give birth but a place where the more experienced women of this community, such as your mother and Marissa Mandocicelli, can offer their practical help and guidance for as long as it's necessary.

'If that type of working model is accepted and embraced by other townships, all the better, but as far as giving me naming rights and recognition for implementing a scheme that has been a part of other cultures for hundreds of years, forget it. I need no such recognition. It's the mothers, babies and volunteer women who are the ones that deserve the praise. I'm just doing my job.'

As she finished talking and let out a breath, Brandon couldn't help but applaud. She was surprised and looked rather sheepish, not used to attracting attention like this. 'Sorry. I do tend to rattle on a bit.' She tucked her hair behind her ear, feeling highly self-conscious as he smiled at her. She shrugged one shoulder shyly and gave him a lopsided grin. 'You should have stopped me.'

'And miss seeing you all fired up and passionate like that! Not a chance.'

'Oh.' She wasn't sure whether that was a compliment or not but decided it was probably best not to dwell on it.

'In fact, now that I've seen that fire burning deep down in your belly...' Even as he started to say the words out loud, Brandon wasn't sure it was a good idea but he didn't seem able to stop himself. 'Would you like to be my partner for the billy-cart race? It's held four days before Christmas. We close off the street again and have a big community Christmas party.'

Clover blinked once then frowned a little. 'A street party? I've never been to one before. Apart from that, I really have no idea what you're talking about, or what my rambling on about a maternity centre has to do with billy-carting. Your mother did mention something about it at dinner but I wasn't really sure what she meant.'

'Yes. That's the race I'm talking about. It's a Christmas tradition in Lewisville, where teams have to build a two-person billy-cart from scraps of wood and metal and rope and things like that, then race them down Main Street.'

'Build?'

'Sure. We'll have time after clinic to design and build a billy-cart.'

'Build?' She was looking at him with utter incredulity. 'I've never built anything in my life.'

Brandon spread his arms wide. 'You built a clinic!'

'Not with my bare hands,' she pointed out. 'I don't know the first thing about how to build a billy-cart.'

'Well, chillax, Clover, because I do. I've been taking part in this race for as long as I can remember. You need to be twelve years or over to enter and I waited *so* long to be old enough.'

'Who did you compete with in your first year?'

'My dad.' Brandon smiled at the memory. 'He was the one who taught me how to build a functioning billy-cart. The wheels, the steering column. Geoffrey and Parker and some of the other guys think that style is the biggest criteria. The flashiest machine. The best paint design.' Brandon shook his head. 'I can clearly remember my father telling me, "Son, straightforward and simple is the best design to have. Everything else is just gravy."'

'How many years have you won?'

His grin grew wider. 'None.'

'None! Then why would I want to be on your team? I thought this race was about a little healthy competition.'

'Ah, see, now, there's that fiery spirit I'm coming to know. Keep that. Harness that as we build our simple but effective *machine of glory.*' Brandon waved his hand in front of him as though announcing a headline. Clover's only answer was to raise an eyebrow.

'So long as you don't call it that.'

He straightened. 'What's wrong with "machine of glory"?'

Clover wrinkled her nose. 'I think we'd better get you out of here. The smell of raw wood and building materials is obviously going to your head.'

Brandon chuckled as they left the maternity centre and headed back next door to Viola's house, Clover gasping once more at the pretty twinkling lights up and down the street. It really was so gorgeously festive, unlike her father's place. Every year a crew came in to erect the four-metre-high Christmas tree exactly one week prior to Christmas and then remove it the day after. Direct. Formal. Clinical.

She shook her head, not wanting to dwell on it. She was having a different sort of Christmas this year and she was going to enjoy it. 'So, has anyone ever been hurt during this race?'

'Oh sure. Last year, we had to forfeit the race because Kurt Shepherd came a cropper and needed medical attention. Broke his right wrist and dislocated his shoulder.'

'Who was your partner last year?' Had he been dating anyone? A girlfriend perhaps? If so, Clover wasn't sure she wanted to hear about it, although she had no idea why.

'Ruby. It was always Dad and I until Ruby joined our family and then Dad would help us build it but Ruby and I would race it.'

'So how do we go about this building thing? Do we need to look at schematics or do some research?' Clover turned to look at him as she spoke and missed her footing on the step, stumbling a little and reaching for the handrail, but it was just out of reach. Crying out in surprise, her hands flailed around for a moment before they connected with something firm and hard—Brandon's arm.

'Whoa! Careful, now,' he remarked as he slid one hand around her waist to steady her, the other reaching for her flailing hands. He caught her in time, hauling her a little closer to him, but at the same time she twisted around and before he realised what was happening, Clover was standing in his arms, facing him, her mouth so incredibly close to his own.

'Sorry. Very clumsy of me,' she remarked.

'Yep.' He smiled.

Disbelief flared momentarily in her eyes. 'You're not supposed to agree with me, Brandon.'

His smile widened into a grin. 'I'm not?'

'No. You're supposed to be gallant and chivalrous.'

'I thought that was what I was doing.' His smile increased. 'But if you want absolute proof...' Before Clover could utter another word, he'd scooped her up off her feet and into his arms. 'How's this?'

'What are you doing?' she protested, heat instantly infusing her entire body at the close contact. 'I'm fine. It was just a little twist. You can put me down.'

'But, you see, chivalry is not dead,' he murmured near her ear as she automatically wound her arms about his neck more for fear that she would fall rather than anything else.

But now that she *was* here, close to his body, the power of his earthy scent teasing its way through her senses, she was going to make the most of it. No man had ever treated her this way before, teasing her yet exciting her all at the same time.

He carried her to the porch swing and set her down gently. Then, kneeling down, he slipped her shoe off the injured foot and with a tenderness that stunned her gently rotated her ankle. 'Does that hurt?' he asked, his tone smooth yet a little deeper than usual.

Could he feel that electrified humming between them? Was he as aware of her as she was of him? How on earth was she supposed to think straight when he was so near, when he was touching her, caring for her? How was it this man could make her forget everything, wiping her mind completely blank, simply by being nice to her?

'Clover?' he asked, when she didn't say anything, and she quickly shook her head, unsure whether she was actually capable of forming words.

She stayed still, noticing he didn't appear to be in any hurry to release her foot. In fact, every time they'd touched in the past, at the wedding when they'd been dancing, afterwards when he'd kissed her cheek or tucked her hair behind her ear; each and every time, he'd been reluctant to break the contact. A small spark of excitement spread throughout her at this knowledge. Brandon was attracted to her. *Really* attracted to her. The knowledge made her bold.

She tipped her head to the side, her hair sliding off her shoulder as she considered him. She swallowed once, twice before deciding to chance her vocal cords, hoping they worked. 'Are you this heroic with every woman you meet?'

A small smile tugged at his lips as his gaze took in the sight of her exposed neck. 'Are you flirting with me, Ms Farraday?'

'That's *Dr* Farraday, if you please, and what if I am?'

Brandon's smile increased and carefully he placed her foot down as though it were the most precious thing in the world. Then, still on bended knee, he leaned forward, angling his words towards her ear, his breath fanning her neck causing goose-bumps to ripple their way down her arm and spine.

'That's a dangerous game to play, *Dr* Farraday, but I'm willing, if you are.'

When he raised his head, there was a challenge in his eyes and Clover's smile increased. 'A game of flirting,' she breathed. 'Something I've never really done before.'

'I find that hard to believe.' His gaze dipped to her lips, lingering there for a moment before meeting her eyes once more. She had to try hard not to gasp or bite her lip as a wave of heat flooded her being. 'Someone as…gorgeous as you?'

'Contrary to what you might believe, Brandon, I've led a very sheltered life.'

'Does that give me an unfair advantage?' Had

he edged closer somehow? Because now when she looked at him, she was positive that if she leaned forward a touch, and if he leaned forward a touch, their lips could finally meet. Was that what she wanted? To be kissed by Brandon? She'd certainly dreamed about it far too many times to count but the fact was she was used to keeping dreams and reality completely separate, not used to her worlds colliding.

'I may,' she breathed softly, 'not know exactly what I'm doing but I'm sure it's hard-wired into my…' she ran her tongue slowly across her bottom lip and was rewarded as a shudder ripped through Brandon, who was now obviously having difficulty swallowing '…system.' The word was barely audible yet it seemed to hang in the air between them.

Neither of them moved. Caught in a bubble in time. What had started out as a simple bit of teasing fun had somehow morphed into something more personal, more intimate. The longer they stayed still, the more she became aware of him.

She wanted to swallow, to breathe, to move, and yet her brain didn't seem to be receiving any signals other than the fact that perhaps, where Brandon was concerned, she'd bitten off more than she could chew.

The man was handsome and sexy, there was no doubt about that, but the way his blue eyes seemed to stare down into her soul, the way his strong arms made her feel more safe and secure than she'd ever felt in her life, the way her heart seemed to beat in time to the rhythm pulsing through him… There was a connection between them, a pure and powerful connection, and she wasn't at all sure she'd be able to resist making that connection physical.

If she angled towards him…just a fraction…

'Brandon!'

At the sound of Viola's voice calling his name, both of them sprang apart, quickly scrambling to their feet. Clover's ankle felt fine as she put weight on it.

'Brandon!' A second later, a breathless Viola came bounding up the steps to the porch, concern and worry etched on her face. 'There you are. And you, too, Clover. Good. There's been an accident.'

CHAPTER FIVE

VIOLA bent forward from the waist, trying to catch her breath. For a split second neither Brandon nor Clover moved, their minds slowly beginning to lift from the sensual fog and return to the real world. She tried hard to ignore the fact that Brandon had been about to kiss her—again. That meant that what she'd felt at the wedding, what she'd spent months dreaming about, wasn't one-sided at all. Brandon was interested in her...but what would his price be?

Two men had come into her life and two men had hurt her when her father had paid them to leave. Would Brandon be so easily bought? Or was he made of sterner stuff? She hoped so. She *really* hoped so. It was a major reason why she needed to keep her Sydney life separate from her time spent in Lewisville.

Brandon led Viola inside and Clover quickly

pulled out a chair from the dining-room table. 'Here. Sit down,' she urged, and helped the woman to sit.

'Take a breath, Mum, then tell us what's happened,' Brandon suggested as he walked to the cupboard in the hall where he knew his sister kept an emergency medical bag packed and ready to go.

He couldn't believe he'd been about to *kiss* Clover! *Again!* What had started out as a harmless bit of teasing, a harmless bit of flirting, had suddenly turned into an awareness so intense he was still nervous deep inside. No woman, not even Lynn, had rocked his world so completely and so easily. He focused his thoughts on whatever had his mother in a tizz.

'I was at Marissa's when she received a call from her niece's cousin, Pamela, saying that two teenage boys in the next-door paddock were playing with the tractors and that they've smashed them and are both hurt. Thankfully they managed to somehow reach one of the UHF radios in the tractors to call for help and this, of course, sent their mother, Susannah, into an absolute tailspin. She couldn't remember what to do and Pamela had just arrived at Susannah's for dinner and couldn't find where the emergency numbers were kept. Anyway, Pamela called Marissa, who lives in town, and then Marissa called Geoffrey, and I said I'd come over here and alert the two of you,' Viola panted.

'Good heavens!' Clover looked from Viola to Brandon. 'What were they doing out on the tractors at this time of night? It's dark!'

'All the more reason to be out as you can see exactly where you're going, especially if you're mucking about.' Brandon shook his head.

Clover shook her head. 'Madness. Total madness.' She patted Viola on the shoulder. 'Breathe, now. We don't need you hyperventilating.'

'Oh, tush. I'm fine. Go and put on a pair of sturdy shoes, girl. Geoffrey and Joan will be here to pick you both up in next to no time.'

'Yes, you're right. As far as police officers go, I have to say he's the most prompt and attentive one I've ever met, and how lucky that he married the town's paramedic.' Clover nodded and headed off to her room. If they were going to be traipsing through paddocks in the dark, socks and lace-up boots were definitely the way to go. She changed out of her three-quarter-length jeans and pulled on a pair of full-length denim ones, nice and comfortable yet sturdy.

She returned and found Brandon talking on the phone, Viola in the kitchen opening drawers and pulling out containers.

'Susannah…Susannah…calm down.' Brandon shook his head, trying to focus on calming down the distraught mother on the other end of the phone, rather than watching Clover as she gathered up her gloriously long hair and tied it back out of the way. He closed his eyes, blocking out the sight of the gorgeous woman. 'OK. Put Pamela on and go and lie down. We're all on our way.'

Clover headed into the kitchen. 'Is he trying to get more information?'

'Yes. Susannah sent the farm manager out to the paddock to be with the boys and to see what's going on. He's just arrived and is relaying messages over the radio and then Pamela's repeating that information to Brandon.'

Clover shook her head in bemusement. 'Another world.' She met Viola's gaze and smiled. 'But a good world, nevertheless.'

Viola nodded, her hands continually busy. 'I knew what you meant, dear.'

'What are you doing?' Clover asked as Viola tipped boiling water into a Thermos.

'Making you and Brandon a relief package. I often do it when he heads out to emergencies like this. Some sandwiches and a flask of coffee. If you don't want them, someone out there will.'

Clover couldn't believe the extent to which this woman continued to give and quickly bent to kiss her cheek. 'You're amazing, Viola. A true mothering kind.'

Viola didn't get a chance to say anything in return as there was the sound of a large vehicle outside and a moment later a deep car horn sounded.

'That's Geoffrey.' Brandon quickly finished his phone call, telling Pamela they were on their way, picked up his medical bag and motioned for Clover to follow him. She held out her hand for the bag Viola had just finished packing, thanked her, then followed Brandon outside.

He opened the front passenger door to Geoffrey's four-wheel-drive, ignoring the way her alluring scent seemed to linger around him. Once she was seated, he closed the door and headed towards Joan, who was driving the ambulance parked behind Geoffrey's police vehicle.

'You're not coming with us in here?' Clover asked through the open window, turning her head to look at him.

'I'll go with Joan. See you there,' he replied, and climbed into the ambulance, a little relieved to have a small reprieve from Clover's enigmatic presence. He was attracted to her. He'd enjoyed flirting with her—far too much—and he knew it was something he could quite easily become addicted to. Having a breather, even if it was only for the twenty minutes it would take to get out to Susannah's property, would be enough time to pull himself together so he could work alongside his alluring colleague.

At least, he hoped it would be enough time.

When they arrived at Susannah's property, they were met by Pamela, who came out to the cars to give them directions to the paddock.

'I'll stay with Susannah. Keep her calm,' Pamela said.

'Does she need medical attention?' Brandon asked. 'Because Joan could pop in now—'

Pamela shook her head. 'No. She's anxious and worried but nothing that requires medical attention. Seeing to her boys will put her mind at rest.'

'Right you are. We'll report our findings via the UHF,' Brandon said, then nodded to Joan. 'Let's head out.' He signalled to Geoffrey and the police officer nodded and put the four-wheel-drive back in motion, its bright spotlights lighting the way through the now dark paddock.

'Just as well it rained three or so hours ago. If the tracks were too muddy, we might have had trouble getting the ambulance out here,' Geoffrey said to Clover.

'This is the wet season now, right? Over Christmas and through until about February?' she asked, glancing in the side-mirror to check that the ambulance was still following them.

'You're correct, Clover. Hot days, a bit of a downpour and coolish nights.'

'And are overturned tractors the normal sort of accidents you might attend out here?'

'Not uncommon but not an everyday occurrence either. Brandon, however, is well versed with Outback medicine so you've nothing to worry about. I have the helicopter on standby and the State Emergency Services are probably about twenty minutes behind us because we'll need their help to right those tractors again.' Geoffrey glanced over at her for a second before returning his attention to the track before him. 'Just thought you might like to know all that because you do look a little anxious.'

'Me? Anxious? Oh, no. Just…interested and… intrigued.' This was so different from her life in Sydney. And so were the feelings that Brandon was stirring inside her. 'While I'm trained as an OB/GYN, I'm more than versed with emergency medicine and it's clear you have everything else under control.'

'Excellent.' Geoffrey guided the car over a cattle grid and pointed towards the group of tractor lights shining in the distance. 'There they are.' He nodded towards the UHF radio. 'Let Brandon and Joan know we're headed off track and to stay close.'

Grinning, Clover picked up the handset. 'I just press the button and talk?'

'Yep. Joan's radio will already be on the emergency frequency.'

She untangled the twisted cord and held the handset to her mouth.

'Uh…um… Brandon? We're going off track. Geoffrey says to stay close.'

'Copy that,' Brandon replied, and where Clover thought that might be the extent of his reply, he continued to talk. 'Been enjoying the drive?' he asked.

'Uh…yes.'

'Good. It's shockingly bumpy in the ambulance.'

'Oi!' they heard Joan protest, and Geoffrey laughed. He motioned for Clover to press the button.

'Stop upsetting my wife,' he told Brandon when Clover held the handset up to his mouth. The police officer was busy bush-bashing his way through the paddock, drawing closer to the lights in the distance.

'She's not your wife, she's my paramedic,' he joked with Geoffrey as they drove through a paddock in the dark, heading towards a serious accident.

'You don't see me upsetting your colleague here,' Geoffrey countered.

'I doubt you'd be able to,' Brandon returned. 'Clover is…unflappable.'

Clover raised her eyebrows at that comment. He thought she was unflappable or was he teasing her again? Had he suggested she go with Geoffrey because the police vehicle had better suspension than the ambulance and therefore she'd be more comfortable? Unfortunately, she had no time to ponder things as Geoffrey was slowing the vehicle down.

Within minutes they were out of the cars, she and Brandon heading towards the tractors while Geoffrey busied himself setting up more lights so they could see what they were doing. Wes, the farm manager, greeted Brandon like an old friend.

'Tyson's not so bad, but Ryan's not too good. He keeps slipping in and out of consciousness but he hasn't stopped breathing.'

'You've done a good job keeping them stable.' Brandon clapped his mate on the shoulder before crouching down beside Ryan, whose legs appeared to be trapped beneath the cab of one of the overturned tractors. Clover had already headed towards Tyson and Joan was bringing over an emergency medical kit from the ambulance. After a brief glance at the tractors, Brandon had quickly summed up what had happened.

'As I suspected. Playing a game of "chicken" with the tractors?' he called to Tyson, his voice holding a strong thread of parental censure but it was clear he didn't really expect an answer.

'Chicken?' Clover asked Joan quietly as she pulled on a pair of gloves and reached for the medical torch so she could check Tyson's pupils, but it was Tyson who answered her, dismay in his tone.

'We race the tractors towards each other and the first one to chicken out and swerve or jump off is the loser.'

'And judging by the state of the tractors, neither of you chickened out?' Clover asked as Joan wound the blood-pressure cuff around Tyson's arm.

'Is…is Ry going to be OK?' Tyson's voice quivered as he spoke.

Clover looked across at where Brandon was bending down next to Ryan's torso, the boy's legs buried beneath the tractor. 'Honestly? I don't know but we'll do everything we can to help him out.' While Clover spoke to Tyson, she continued to check his vital signs. 'Cognitive function is good. Pupils are equal and reacting to light. You've got a large scratch on your head where you've banged it but I don't think it'll need suturing. Let's get you cleaned up and then I'll know more.'

'Respiratory rate and blood pressure are both elevated but still within normal range,' Joan reported.

'Where exactly does it hurt, Tyson?' Clover asked.

'My right shoulder,' he stated, and Clover instantly felt his shoulder. Tyson yelped in pain.

'Feels dislocated. I'd like it X-rayed before it's relocated to check there's no fracture to the neck of humerus. IV line, ten milligrams of morphine for the pain, stabilise his shoulder, cervical collar, clean and bandage the head wound. I'll assess him before transfer to see if further analgesics are required.'

While she spoke, Clover continued to check Tyson's other arm and his leg bones, checking reflexes to make sure everything else was in order.

'You've been very lucky,' she told Tyson, before pulling off her gloves and reaching for another pair from Joan's medical kit. 'I'll go help Brandon,' she said and left Tyson in Joan's more than capable hands.

'What have we got?' she asked Brandon as she knelt down beside Ryan, who was breathing through a non-rebreather oxygen mask. Clover bent down even further to peer beneath the tractor's cab to try and see what was happening with Ryan's legs.

'He's roused once but wasn't able to articulate exactly where he felt pain. I've set up a drip and have administered a dose of morphine and Maxolon.'

As he spoke, he held out his hand towards Geoffrey, who was walking towards them, a bag of plasma in his hand and another portable stand. 'Thanks, mate,' he said to Geoffrey, then turned to continue with his set-up. 'The plasma drip will help replace the blood loss.'

Clover assisted him, the two working effortlessly together. 'Blood pressure is low so between the plasma and saline we'll boost his fluids, pupils are reacting to light but sluggish. Pulse is slower. He's holding but until we can get the tractor off him, there's not much we can do.'

'Once it's shifted, though, we'll have to move fast,' Clover added, looking behind her at the cab. 'There's a high risk of toxins building up in his blood due to crush syndrome. It's clear he's losing blood so we'll need to tie off the offending arteries and stabilise him as quickly as possible. I'll be ready to intubate and resuscitate if required.'

'Good.' Brandon watched her, noticing she was

completely focused. 'Are you OK, Clover? Bit different from Sydney, hey?'

'It is, but I'm here to help and ready to do whatever is necessary to ensure Ryan pulls through with flying colours.' She smiled. 'As you've trained in emergency procedures and as this is *your* town, you take the lead and I'll be your lackey.'

'My lackey?' Brandon raised an interested eyebrow.

'For this emergency,' she clarified as they finished setting up the plasma drip. 'Once we have him stabilised, what happens next?'

'Geoffrey will organise for the helicopter to land somewhere close by.'

'Out here? In the paddock?'

'It's flat enough and that means we don't have to transport the boys back into Lewisville. They can go straight onto the chopper and be transferred to Broken Hill Base Hospital, where Ryan will no doubt undergo orthopaedic surgery, possibly microsurgery, depending on how bad his fractures are.'

Brandon looked up towards Geoffrey, who,

with Wes's help, had finished setting up some bright spotlights, providing more than enough illumination for when they finally shifted the cab from Ryan's legs. 'How much longer for the SES?'

'Two minutes. They radioed in to say they can see us in the distance.'

'They could see us in outer space, mate. Good work on the lights.' He looked over at Joan. 'How's Tyson?'

'Blood pressure stabilising. Vital signs improving.'

'Good. Get him as stable as possible so Wes can monitor him because we'll need you over here once we lift this cab off Ryan's legs.'

'OK,' Joan answered.

'Ready for the chopper?' Geoffrey asked.

'Ready,' Brandon confirmed.

'I can hear those SES trucks in the distance,' Clover remarked, and began checking Ryan's vital signs again, managing to rouse him once more but still not for long. 'His breathing is stable, pupils have no change from before. His blood pressure is still low. I wouldn't be surprised if the femoral artery's been damaged.'

'Agreed.'

'I'll get that intubation and resuscitation equipment ready.' Clover went to stand but Geoffrey was by her side in an instant.

'What do you need?' he asked, and she told him what supplies she'd require from the ambulance. 'You have him well trained,' she called to Joan, clearly impressed.

'I heard that,' Geoffrey retorted, and they all smiled. He returned a moment later with the equipment Clover required, then went to direct the SES trucks, which were now almost upon them. Together, she and Brandon continued to prepare, pleased when after five minutes of the drip and plasma doing their jobs Ryan's blood pressure was slowly beginning to rise.

'He's better stabilised now for what's about to happen. Ideally, I'd prefer to give him a spinal block but, given the circumstances, perhaps morphine, five milligrams, every five to ten minutes.'

'Agreed,' Clover said, even though she wasn't sure whether Brandon had been asking a question. She wanted him to know he could rely on her, that she was ready to work alongside him. Geoffrey and the SES captain came over, Brandon greeting him warmly.

'I'm Alistair.' He waved briefly at Clover. 'I'd heard we had a new doctor in town. Terrible circumstances for a first meeting.'

'True, but I'm pleased to meet you in any case. We appreciate the assistance you and your crew will be providing.' She smiled up at Alistair and Brandon watched as the SES captain became instantly enamoured with her.

Jealousy sliced through Brandon and he quickly pushed it away. He couldn't deny not only his attraction to Clover but that they made a great team.

'Have we got everything we need?' Clover asked, peering into the medical bag. 'Locking forceps? Sutures? Swabs? Bandages? Or do I need to get some stuff from the ambulance?'

'We need all those things. If you can get it organised, I'll take Ryan's vital signs again.' Brandon worked calmly and methodically alongside Clover.

This was the first time in a very long time that she'd attended an emergency where someone wasn't giving birth and, as such, she was having to draw on her long-term memory to recall exactly what the procedure was, which was why she was relying on Brandon to direct her in this particular matter.

'Chopper will be here in under five,' Geoffrey reported.

'Excellent,' Brandon responded, then called to Joan, 'How's Tyson?'

'His vital signs are improving. BP is now back to normal,' Joan added.

'Good.'

Alistair's tone blended with Brandon's as he gave instructions to his men. 'Right, lads, get those cables secure. Dunfield, you're on the winch. Peterson, get that flame retardant flowing. Jones, have you finished your assessment?' Alistair shifted around to the other side of the tractor's cab to have a look.

Clover headed to the ambulance, quite impressed with all the activity. When she returned with the supplies still in the sterile packaging, she set them out on a tray, eager to get the job done in order to save Ryan's life. Their patients were all that mattered now and both she and Brandon knew that once the tractor had been shifted, they'd need to work quickly to avoid Ryan bleeding out.

'Ready?' Alistair called a while later.

Brandon looked at Clover and their eyes locked. He held her gaze before nodding once questioningly. She immediately nodded back. 'Ready,' he confirmed.

As they had suspected, once the SES workers elevated the cab, righting the tractor, the need to work precisely yet swiftly was on them. As though they'd worked together all their lives, Clover and Brandon were able to find the ruptured femoral artery and clamp it off, while checking the fractured right femur, tibia and fibula for other possible problems.

'The left leg is fractured but just the tib and fib,' Clover confirmed. 'The fracture looks more like a jigsaw that will require careful piecing together,' she remarked, as they debrided the wound and stabilised the fractures as best they could.

Brandon temporarily sutured off the femoral artery before he packed and bandaged the leg, splinting it and readying Ryan for transfer to the helicopter, which had landed nearby. Geoffrey and one of the other SES workers had already transferred Tyson, who was now being monitored by Joan. There was the sound of a car approaching and Clover glanced over her shoulder to see Pamela pulling a car to a halt, then climbing out and helping another woman from the car, a woman who started sobbing as soon as she saw the boys.

'Your mum's here, Ryan,' Brandon told the boy, who opened his eyes for a moment and mumbled something before closing his eyes again.

'Good response,' Clover said softly. 'Listening and acknowledging. Shows excellent cognitive function.'

After Ryan had been transferred, Brandon helped Clover into the helicopter as Joan climbed out, Susannah already secured in the front seat next to the pilot, a bag of clothes at her feet.

'I'll drive to Broken Hill straight away,' Pamela was telling her friend. 'Brandon will help you.

Just…stay calm. The boys are going to be fine. Isn't that right, Doc?' she called.

'They'll pull through,' Brandon confirmed.

Clover looked from Brandon to the puffy-eyed woman in the front seat, who was wearing a set of headphones with a microphone attached. Clover put on her own headphones and started to strap herself in, ready for take-off. Brandon was thanking Geoffrey, Joan, Wes and the crew before the police officer bent his head, the chopper's blades starting to whirl around as he ensured the door was securely closed.

'Susannah,' Clover said into the microphone, 'can you hear me? It's Clover…er…Dr Farraday.'

'Uh…yes?' Susannah replied, and looked around behind her to where Clover was sitting. Clover waved as Geoffrey came around to ensure Susannah's door was securely closed before signalling to the pilot that he was ready for take-off.

Clover was aware of Brandon sitting down beside her and strapping himself in and donning a pair of headphones, but it was Susannah who mattered right at this moment. The mother of the two teenage boys was clearly distressed and Clover knew that when they arrived at the hospital Susannah would need to be calm and lucid for when the surgeons not only explained the procedures to her but required her to authorise the surgery.

'Your boys are doing very well. Tyson has been conscious the whole time, talking to us and helping us to understand what happened. At the moment, though, we've given him something for the pain to help his body begin the recovery process. I know what they did was wrong, playing with the tractors like that, but what I need you to focus on is that they're both all right. Ryan's injuries are a little more extensive than Tyson's but, given time, he'll pull through and will be back to causing mischief in no time.'

At these words Clover was rewarded with a small laugh from the mother. Susannah hiccupped a few more times but thankfully, for now, the tears seemed to have stopped.

Clover continued talking to Susannah, explaining some of the procedures and protocols that would happen when they landed at the hospital and what the surgeons would say to her. Susannah, while still distraught her sons would require surgical intervention, was at least able to accept that fact and asked Clover a few questions.

Brandon listened to what Clover was saying while monitoring the boys, ensuring their vital signs were stable. Clover's tone of voice was one of calm assurance and where Susannah had been an emotional wreck when she'd entered the helicopter, by the time they arrived at Broken Hill Base Hospital, she appeared far more in control and ready to be a parent to her boys. Clover was a complete natural, putting everyone at ease.

Brandon introduced Clover to the hospital staff and they stayed with Susannah while the two teenagers headed off to Radiology.

'Will you stay with me when the surgeon comes to explain things?' Susannah asked Clover, almost clinging to her.

'Of course we will.' Clover turned to look at Brandon, who instantly nodded. He was in awe of the way she'd been able to calm Susannah, the way she supported the mother and the way both teenage boys, after returning from X-Ray, seemed to smile almost shyly whenever Clover paid them the slightest bit of attention. He'd never met anyone like her.

The woman with the long, luscious locks and big brown eyes had the most encompassing smile he'd ever seen. Was it her calm and empowering voice that set people at ease? Was it the words she used? Was it the way she carried herself? The natural way that Clover communicated with everyone took his breath away.

The woman before him was a calm and controlled doctor, who had handled the emergency with professionalism and grace. How she managed a clear mix of the two he had no idea but her ability to put anyone at ease, her soothing voice and natural charm was enough to make people promise her the moon, should she ask for it.

Brandon continued to watch her surreptitiously as she carried on charming those around her. Lynn had used her charms, had used her feminine wiles to lie and cheat her way into his heart. She'd told him she was a freelance journalist, travelling around, writing stories about the true Aussie Outback hero. She'd written an article on Ned Finnegan and how being mayor of an Outback community was different from being an inner-city politician, and when she'd decided to do a piece on the local doctors, she'd fixated on him.

Brandon had been taken with her clever words, her turn of phrase and the way she showed him she was definitely interested right from the start. She'd been in town for several months, the two of them becoming incredibly close, when he'd started to think about proposing. Lynn was everything he'd ever wanted in a lifelong partner and she'd appeared to love Lewisville, still travelling around, stopping at some of the outlying homesteads to do more research and gather more stories.

Turned out she'd gathered more than just stories, especially when he'd headed out to the Palmers' farm for an emergency case and discovered Lynn had been sleeping with one of the jackaroos.

When he'd confronted her, she hadn't denied it.

'It's too late, Brandon.' She'd spread her arms wide. 'Jamie and I are leaving tomorrow.'

'Were you going to tell me or just…disappear?'

His hands had clenched into fists as he'd tried to control his emotions.

She'd shrugged. 'Disappear. It's cleaner, easier that way. Jumpin' Jamie's been offered a job at one of the theme parks in Queensland, riding horses and crackin' whips! Yee-ha!' She'd fanned her face and smiled seductively. 'Ooh, that man is hot! And things will be even hotter than here on the sunny Gold Coast. Beaches! Oh, how I've missed beaches!'

'But, Lynn...?' He hadn't been able to believe the woman he'd given his heart to was indeed a heartless, cheating, lying vixen. 'This can't be the real you. Where's the woman who loved watching the sun set? Or sitting quietly on the porch swing, enjoying the peace and quiet? Or joining in with the bush dances and being involved with the community?'

Lynn had spread her arms wide. 'Gone. This is the real me, Brandon. I thought for a moment there that I could have been something else...and then I met Jamie and realised that porch swings and quilting bees were *so* not who I am.'

'And Jamie? Is it serious with him?'

She'd laughed. 'What? No way. I'm not the set-tling-down kind of girl. He'll do…for a while.' Then she'd sauntered over to him and run her fingernail down his cheek. 'Until I find some-one to replace him with.'

Brandon had stood his ground, disgust slowly replacing the love he'd felt for her. 'Was any of it real?' he'd asked softly.

Lynn had taken a step back and met his eyes fair and square, whispering one simple word in his direction. 'No.'

In the distance, someone coughed, bringing Brandon out of his reverie. He looked at Clover as she smiled at someone. He couldn't shake the thought that she was still hiding something. He was positive of it. Something deep and im-portant, something that answered all the ques-tions he had and yet somehow, when it was just the two of them, he found himself forgetting all those questions, caught up in the moment, in her eyes, wanting desperately to touch her long, flowing hair.

'Is any of it real?' he whispered to himself,

then shook his head, knowing that where personal matters of the heart were concerned, he'd be a fool to let himself become involved with Clover.

CHAPTER SIX

THANKFULLY, they didn't have to wait around too long for the helicopter pilot to give them a ride back to Lewisville.

'What now?' Clover asked as they watched the chopper return to the sky and fly off into the night. Brandon pointed to the ambulance, which was garaged near the helipad.

'We can drive the ambulance back to town. Park it at the clinic for the night.'

'How far is Lewisville from here?'

'A ten-minute walk.'

'Oh, well, it's ridiculous to take the ambulance for such a short distance,' she remarked. 'It's a lovely night, a definite breeze in the air, so I vote we walk.'

'Sounds good.' Brandon shoved his hands into his pockets as they started walking back to town. He'd continued to watch Clover at the hospital, his intrigue increasing with every passing moment he spent with her. He'd noticed that she appeared genuine enough when she was with patients, really wanting to help them, but what about Outback life in general? Did she like it? Would she be like Lynn and say one thing but mean another? He decided to try digging a little. 'So…what do you think of Lewisville?'

Her smile was immediate. 'I love it. The community, the way everyone pulls together, the stars you can see in the sky.' She waved her hand upwards as though to prove it. 'It's like its own little world, so far away from the toxicity of the city.'

'You're not a city girl?'

Clover laughed without humour, then sighed. 'I'm not sure I know *what* sort of girl I am.'

'But you've lived in the city all your life?'

'Yes.' That was all she said and was silent for a moment before changing the subject. Right on cue, he thought as he listened to her talk about how pretty the town was at Christmastime. It was definitely clear that she really didn't like to talk about her life in Sydney and he was becoming more and more curious why.

What had happened to her? Why didn't she get along with her father? Did she have any siblings? Was she married but running away from her past? She didn't wear any rings but that didn't mean anything.

'I do like it here, though,' she continued, still talking about the town. 'And I especially can't wait for this billy-cart race. When do we start with all the hammering and sawing and stuff?'

'Clover, are you married?'

His question stunned her so much she stopped walking and stared at him. Although there were plenty of stars in the night sky, shining down with the help from the half-moon, there wasn't enough light for her to see Brandon's expression properly but she could tell from the tone of his voice that he was serious.

'No,' she replied after a pause. She started walking again. 'Where does the billy-cart construction take place? In the shed out the back of your mother's house?'

'Why don't you like talking about your life? Opening up? Sharing?'

'Why don't you?' she countered, still heading towards the town. Brandon spread his arms wide.

'In this town? You only need to ask the nearest resident to be told all my gossip.'

Clover shook her head. 'I don't listen to gossip.'

'Neither do I, which means we've both been gossiped about in the past. Right?'

'You could say that.' She thought of the media who would often surround her father wherever he went. He was used to it, though, encouraging it to a point. In fact, she'd often felt he had a better relationship with the media than he did with his own daughter. She shook her head, clearing away thoughts of her father.

They continued to walk on but Clover seemed more than happy not to question him further. 'You're really not going to ask.'

'About?'

'About my past.'

'I'm more than happy to listen if you want to talk. If not, I'm more than capable of making up my own mind about your personality and character from what I've observed.'

'And what's that?'

Clover's smile was instant. 'Fishing?'

'Well, when a beautiful woman is forming an opinion of me, naturally I'm going to want to know what she thinks. Curiosity is part of human nature.'

'OK, then. I think you're an amazing doctor, which was proved tonight with the way you treated Ryan and Tyson. You genuinely care for the community at large, pitching in and helping out wherever necessary, whether it be manning a roadside tent when Main Street is blocked off, hanging twinkle lights or judging a bake-off competition.'

'Hey, I thought you said you didn't listen to gossip.'

'It wasn't gossip. Your mother was showing me some of the awards she's won for her delicious goodies and happened to mention that sometimes you were one of the judges.'

Brandon preened a little. 'It's a tough job but someone's got to do it.' Clover laughed, the sweet tinkling sound washing over him and warming his heart. 'Especially if Marissa Mandocicelli's entering.' He kissed his fingers. *'Delizioso!'*

'Did I mention how modest you are?' she added teasingly, and they both chuckled. 'You've already told me you don't like untruths, which means someone has lied to you in a big way. It's clear the way you're desperate to find out about me that you've been duped in the past, no doubt by a woman who broke your heart.'

'I thought she'd broken it,' he said as they turned the corner and began walking down the bitumen road on the outskirts of the town. 'Now I'm not so sure.'

'Really?'

'Clover, I almost kissed you again tonight.'

'Uh…um…right.' His blunt delivery caused her heart to flutter and she wasn't at all sure how to react to such forward statements. When she glanced at him, she could see he was smiling and wasn't sure whether that was good or bad.

'You're easily flustered. It's a nice, endearing quality, which I'm starting to realise is quite genuine.'

'You thought I was pretending?' When he didn't answer, she nodded knowingly. 'Because you've been hurt, you have to question everything. Everyone new to your life already starts off with three strikes against them until they can prove otherwise.'

He shrugged but didn't deny it. 'Call it an unfortunate byproduct of being lied to.'

'Did she cheat on you?'

'How…could you know that?'

'It was a guess but a calculated one as infidelity is one of the major causes for relationship breakdown.'

Brandon shrugged, deciding if he wanted to know more about Clover, perhaps if he opened up, she'd do the same. 'Lynn cheated, yes. I was getting ready to propose and she was getting ready to leave with another man. She said Lewisville wasn't for her, too boring, where nothing exciting ever really happened.'

'Where is she now?'

He shrugged. 'She was headed to Queensland from here, to the coast.'

'Was she a doctor?'

'No. A journalist.'

Clover couldn't help the shudder that passed

through her but, thankfully, Brandon didn't seem to notice.

'You sound as though you know a lot about relationship breakdown. Any bad relationships in your past?'

Clover thought about this for a moment as they neared the town. 'Of the romantic variety?'

Brandon nodded.

'I can't say there have been any good ones.' She thought about the pointed look in her father's eyes when she'd confronted him about buying off her last boyfriend.

'Dad! You can't do this. You can't control my life in this way and pay them never to see me again. This is the second time you've done this. It's not fair.'

'Life isn't fair, Clover.' His tone had been disinterested as he'd perused a pile of spreadsheets. 'I offered them money. They took it. It's not my fault they didn't "love" you. I've done you a huge favour. Now at least you know they were only interested in you for your money and nothing else.'

Oswald had picked up the phone to make a call, glancing up at his daughter. 'It's part of being a Sampson. Everyone always wants something from you and everyone always has a price. Get used to it.'

He'd made his call, ignoring the way she'd stood there for another few minutes before she'd stormed to her room, weeping into her pillow when she'd realised he'd been right. It appeared everyone did have their price and as long as she was known to be a Sampson, people always would. It was during that long and lonely night that Clover had decided to change her name. After all, she'd been twenty-two years old, about to finish medical school, and if she didn't want people taking advantage of her for the rest of her life, then she'd do her best to hide her true identity. So she'd taken her mother's maiden name—Farraday—as her own, and she'd graduated from medical school as plain and simple Clover Farraday, as opposed to Clover Farraday-Sampson, heiress to the Sampson empire.

'What about your dad?' Brandon knew he was treading on unstable ground. 'You mentioned the two of you don't get along?'

She was silent for a minute and at first he

thought she was going to ignore his question completely but finally she said softly, 'My father only knows I exist when I excel so as a child I tried to excel at everything in order to get his attention.' She shook her head, wondering what Oswald would make of his daughter up and leaving Sydney to spend three months in the Outback. Would he even care?

'After my mother passed away, things became worse. He threw himself into work and I was pushed even more into the background. I slowly became accustomed to being passed over, having him forget my birthdays, packing me off to boarding school so he didn't have to deal with me.'

'Clover...' Brandon frowned, his tone intense and sympathetic. 'I'm really sorry to hear that.'

Clover shrugged. 'I coped. Studying medicine helped a lot and, of course, I worked hard in order to get top marks in an attempt to impress him.'

'Did it work?'

'He scanned my grades then looked me directly in the eyes for a whole five seconds and said, "As expected," before moving on to the next item on his agenda.'

'Wow. That's harsh. What on earth does he do for a job? Is he a lawyer or something?'

'Or something,' Clover grumbled as they walked towards his mother's house, the town in darkness now as the twinkle lights had long since clicked off. They slowed their pace, both of them stopping at the steps leading up to the house. 'I don't want to talk about my past.' She sighed and looked around the quiet town. 'I just want to enjoy spending time in Lewisville over the next three months.'

'You're not missing the big city?'

Clover shook her head. 'Not at all. Sydney is just where I'm based.' She looked up at Brandon and shrugged one shoulder, her gaze holding his. 'I've yet to find where I belong.'

Brandon swallowed as he stared into her gorgeous eyes. Although it was dark, his eyes had long since adjusted to the lack of light and he could have sworn he saw the smallest hint of desperation in her face. Certainly he heard it in her voice.

'Aren't we all?' He placed a hand on the rail and gripped it tightly, trying to control the urge to pull her into his arms and wipe away all her uncertainty. The need to save, the need to help, the need to protect the woman before him was becoming too strong to fight—and she'd been back in Lewisville for less than one day.

The attraction he'd felt the first time they'd met had burst to life within minutes of their meeting. He'd thought it was ridiculous and as she'd only been passing through town he'd rationalised that it was OK for him to move fast. Now that she was here for another few months, he simply *had* to slow things down.

He'd rushed into his relationship with Lynn and he'd been burned. He *had* to learn from his past mistakes and, given that prior to tonight's emergency he'd been about to press his lips to Clover's, it would be best for both their sakes if they kept their relationship professional but friendly. Working together, being polite and, of course, constructing a billy-cart together.

'Anyway,' he said, and took a giant step back from his mother's house, 'we'd best get to bed.'

His eyes widened at his words. 'Separately, I mean. You to yours.' He pointed to his mother's house. 'Me to mine.' He jerked a thumb over his shoulder to indicate towards his unit down the street.

Clover smiled. 'I knew what you meant. Clinic in about…' she checked her watch '…five hours.'

'Right.' He rubbed his hands together and then shoved them into his pockets. 'Lots of patients. Especially for you. First full day consulting and I think your clinic is already bursting at the seams.'

'Excellent news. While I'm in town, best to put my skills to use.'

They both stood there. Staring. Not moving. Barely breathing. Their gazes trained upon each other. Their fingers itching to reach out and touch. Their mouths going dry as they did their best to ignore the irrepressible tug of desire zinging through the air around them.

Clover was wondering just how much longer she could stand it and as she shifted her feet, wanting nothing more than to draw closer to him, Brandon took another step back, effectively putting more distance between them.

'Well…' He started walking slowly backwards down the street, his eyes still on her. 'See you later on this morning.'

Clover swallowed and nodded, forcing a polite smile. 'Absolutely.' Her erratic heart rate started to settle, the more distance he put between them. 'Bright and early.'

'At the clinic,' he confirmed.

'Big day.' She climbed up a few steps, still facing him, wanting to keep watching him for as long as possible. As she took another step, the sensor light came on and she blinked, startled. She held up a hand to block it so she could still see him, but while her eyes readjusted, she could hear his warm, sensual laughter floating over her.

'It's a little bright, isn't it?' he remarked, his tone now coming from down the street.

'Just a bit.' She returned his laughter. 'Good night, Brandon.'

'Good night, Clover.'

And as she walked towards the front door, she paused, watching his shadow retreat down the street until she could see him no more.

Heading inside, she tiptoed towards her bedroom, desperate not to wake Viola by tripping over something. In her room, she didn't immediately turn on the light. Instead, she headed to the window and peered out the lacy curtains to see if she could see him but was out of luck. No doubt he was already opening the door to his unit, going inside and forgetting all about her.

She hoped he wasn't and as she brushed her teeth and prepared for sleep, she wondered if she'd finally found the one man who was indeed right for her.

What would happen when she eventually told him about her father? About exactly whose daughter she was? About her family fortune? Would it make a difference? Would he be able to accept her for who she was rather than for what he could get from her? Would he also have his price? Was Brandon a man who could be bought? She desperately hoped not.

Brandon headed inside his unit but didn't switch on the light, moving easily around the place in the dark. He kicked off his shoes and lay back on his unmade bed. He'd tossed and turned last night, wondering what would happen when

Clover returned to Lewisville, and now he had his answer. The fact that the attraction between them appeared to be still very much alive was something he'd just have to deal with.

Moving slow was of paramount importance. It was clear she was hiding something, not wanting to talk about her past or her childhood. All he knew about her was that she'd developed the maternity centre in the Blue Mountains and had applied the same model to a centre down in Tathra. Now she was here, helping him out with his clinic for the next three months. What would she be doing once her time here was finished? Setting up another clinic somewhere else? Helping other people?

She was definitely a giving person, wanting to focus on other people rather than herself. Surely that was a good sign. Then again, Lynn had seemed to be the same way when she'd first arrived in town, wanting to write articles on the townsfolk, making them feel special and wanted.

Then, of course, it had transpired that she'd been playing them all, stringing them along until she'd secured her story. She'd pretended to enjoy the quilting bees, the little community events, the close relationship she'd shared with him before she'd ripped his heart out with her lies and deception.

Was Clover the same? Was she just saying she was looking for a place to belong to be polite? It hadn't seemed that way, especially with that slight hint of need and longing in her tone. Then again, she might be an even more accomplished actress than Lynn—but he hoped not. He really hoped not.

CHAPTER SEVEN

'THAT sounds like a great idea, Ned.' Brandon walked from his consulting room to the reception area with Ned Finnegan, the mayor of Lewisville, as the man continued to chatter about the Christmas street party and billy-cart events due to take place just before Christmas.

Clover had been in town now for two weeks and each day he was finding it more and more difficult to keep his distance, to look upon her as merely another colleague. To say she was brilliant with the patients was an understatement and along with his mother, Marissa and Ned's wife, May, the maternity centre programmes were up and running.

He'd already received feedback from the women of the community, each of them not only extolling the virtues of the support but also giving glowing reports about Clover.

'She's so natural and genuine with everyone,' one woman said.

'So giving. She really wants to help, to make sure we can cope,' another reported.

On a professional level Brandon was pleased to hear such reports, but on a personal level it only drew him closer to the woman he wasn't sure he should get involved with. To hear people saying she was natural and genuine should have promoted confidence in him but instead it only made him more cautious.

Everyone had taken to Lynn like a duck to water, eager to involve her in the community, and look what had happened there. She'd duped them all and left the town without a word of goodbye. Therefore it was impossible for him to let go so easily, to trust again so quickly, and with the way Clover played her cards close to her chest, caution was still his main theme.

'By the way,' Ned continued, raising his voice to combat the loud crying from little two-year-old Ryder in the waiting room. 'How are things going with your billy-cart? Construction should be completed sooner rather than later,' Ned went on, barely stopping to draw breath. 'I was so happy to hear you'd asked Clover to be your partner. A great way to involve her in the community. Anyway, as mayor, don't forget I still need to sight your final billy-cart design.'

Brandon nodded. He'd been dragging his heels where the billy-cart was concerned as he was hesitant to be alone with Clover. Talking, discussing, building. He'd asked her on a whim, wanting to do exactly as Ned had suggested and get her involved to see how she fared, but now, given the fact that his dreams about her were becoming more intense, he wasn't sure he'd made the right decision.

'I'll get them to you soon.'

'Tomorrow,' Ned said pointedly, raising his voice again to combat little Ryder's loud crying. The toddler's poor mother, Tan, was trying desperately to calm him down but the child refused to listen.

Just then, Clover came out of her consulting room, talking to her patient, a bright smile on her face. Brandon ignored the way his gut immediately tightened at the sight of her. She was his colleague and it was imperative he maintain a professional distance.

She was dressed in flat shoes, a dark pencil skirt, which came to mid-thigh, and a cream shirt with short capped sleeves. Her long, luscious brown hair was clipped back at the nape of her neck. She wore little make-up and a pair of simple gold studs in her ears. She was...classically stunning.

Today she was the demure professional. At the wedding she'd been the sexy temptress, causing him to have wild dreams about her...dreams that had only become more intense since she'd arrived in Lewisville. He was glad he no longer lived at home, more than happy to be sleeping in his little unit situated at the rear of the clinic.

To have to sleep under the same roof as Clover, to be in the next bedroom, to hear her moving around, sharing a bathroom...that would have made his attraction towards her even more difficult to fight.

Ned tapped him on the arm and Brandon instantly turned his attention back to the mayor, unable to believe he'd simply been standing there, staring at Clover. 'So don't forget. Designs by tomorrow.'

'Er...Ned...' Brandon began, but Ned was already talking to Joan, the clinic's receptionist-cum-paramedic.

'Hello,' Brandon heard Clover say, and he returned his attention to her, watching in astonishment as she sat down on the floor in the middle of the waiting room, giving little Ryder her full attention. Ryder, however, gave her none of his, still intent on having his temper tantrum.

'I can scream louder than you,' Clover remarked, and in the next instant she tipped her head back and let go with an extraordinarily loud scream.

Everyone in the waiting room stared in stunned disbelief, half of them covering their ears as she continued to yell. After ten seconds Ryder stopped and sat up from where he'd been lying on the floor at his mother's feet. Clover finished her yell then shrugged, not looking at anyone but the little boy who was staring at her in complete puzzlement as though to say, *Grown-ups aren't supposed to act like that!*

'Do you like my long hair?' she asked him, and unclipped the gorgeous locks, dragging a handful across her shoulder and shaking it in front of Ryder. Like a cat with a piece of string, the child was unable to resist and clamped his chubby hand around the glorious locks. He gave a good tug on it but Clover didn't seem to mind. Instead, she held out her hands to him. The toddler clearly forgot he'd been in the middle of a tantrum. 'Let's go into my room and play.'

Without another word and with his hand still securely around her hair, he leaned towards her and she picked him up, rising from the floor with poise and grace. As she walked towards her consulting room, she kept her attention focused on Ryder, talking softly to him. Ryder's bemused mother followed, shaking her head in disbelief.

However, before Clover closed her door, she glanced at Brandon then, without a word, angled her head sharply, beckoning him to follow her. It took half a second for Brandon's sluggish brain to receive the message and with a slight frown but an incredible amount of interest he headed for her room, closing the door behind him.

'I'll keep Master Ryder quiet while you examine him,' she remarked, her tone calm and controlled before she sat on the examination couch, Ryder on her lap. The toddler was staring at her as though still completely unsure how he was supposed to react to such a strange lady.

'I know how you feel, kid,' Brandon mumbled, before asking Tan why they'd come to the clinic.

'I was clearing up after lunch and he was playing in his room and then he just started screaming and clutching his head.'

'*How* did he clutch his head?' Brandon asked.

'I don't understand.' Tan looked at him, confused.

'Were his hands around his jaw? Around his ears? Over his eyes?'

'Uh…' Tan thought for a moment. 'His ears,' she announced with triumph.

'Right.' Brandon walked to Clover's desk, picked up her otoscope and slid a new plastic shield into place on the tip. He glanced at Clover, who was still somehow mesmerising Ryder with her long hair.

'We'll check his ears first,' he said, and leaned

closer, highly aware of the summery scent surrounding Clover. Why did she have to smell so good? Being this close to her had the tantalising effect of heightening his awareness. His arm accidentally brushed hers and he actually pulled back at the contact, their gazes meshing and holding for a split second, as though both had felt that strange undercurrent that seemed to flow between them.

'Angle his head.' Brandon hadn't meant his words to come out so gruff but he didn't have time to worry about that. He needed to switch off his unbidden attraction to his colleague and focus on their little patient. Cradling the boy closer, Clover twisted her own body so Ryder was in the correct position for Brandon's examination.

'Ah,' he said a moment later, and pulled back, taking two huge steps away from the couch and almost bumping into Clover's desk, so desperate was he to put a bit of distance between them. 'He has a very small object in his ear. I'm not exactly sure what it is.'

'What?' Tan was astonished. 'But how? Why? You mean wax, right?'

'No. It's like a small toy or a pebble or something like that,' Brandon continued, and walked to the supply cupboard, pulling out a few different bits and pieces. Clover watched as he focused on the task at hand, obviously wanting to ignore that brief frisson that had passed between them. Perhaps that was the wisest course of action, especially when they were at work.

She'd been in Lewisville for two weeks now and to say they had been some of the best weeks of her life was an understatement. However, since her first eventful evening when Brandon had almost kissed her on the porch swing, things had cooled between them. She was still highly aware of him and she still found herself waking in the mornings, her dreams full of thoughts of the two of them together, but Brandon had definitely put on the brakes. She couldn't—and didn't—blame him. Someone had to be strong out of the two of them and she was glad it was him.

They were colleagues and it was better if they maintained a professional attitude towards each other, rather than cuddling close, dancing and kissing, as they'd done back at the wedding.

Her days had been filled with patients and clinics and getting programmes up and running at the maternity centre. The word that an OB/GYN was now working in Lewisville seemed to have been spread far and wide and she was not only seeing women from the district of Hueyton but beyond.

Working in the clinic and filling in for Ruby in a general practice capacity also gave Clover the opportunity to treat a wide variety of patients, such as little Ryder here. She watched as Brandon pulled out a pair of alligator forceps, a kidney dish and a mild anaesthetic spray.

Working with Brandon, being near him, seeing him every day at work, was internally thrilling, not only as she admired his clever hands or the way he would smile at a patient, instantly putting them at ease, but also in a practical way where the clinic was concerned. If a decision needed to be made, Brandon simply made it. There was no need to write a proposal, to submit letters to the hospital board for approval, to be bound by mounds of red tape as she'd been for so many years working at a larger institution.

It was glorious. *He* was glorious, and she'd come to admire him as a professional colleague... as well as a handsome man. He was still the last person she'd thought about before drifting off to sleep, dreaming of him...dancing with him... being held close, having him kiss her cheek, her eyes, her neck...her mouth.

Clover looked away, annoyed with herself for daydreaming again—and right in front of him, too. He was busy securing a head mirror in place to help him see more clearly into Ryder's ear canal and after pulling on a pair of gloves he appeared ready to begin. She swallowed, glancing at him again, desperate to control the telltale blush she could feel starting to spread across her cheeks.

'Tan...' Brandon's deep, rich tone washed over Clover, causing a delighted shiver to race down her spine. She swallowed, keeping her gaze firmly focused on entertaining the toddler. 'We're going to need to give Ryder a mild sedative as I don't think even Clover, with her hypnotising hair, is going to be able to keep Ryder still enough while I remove the object. He'll be awake the whole time,' he quickly reassured her. 'Just drowsy and not really knowing what's going on. The sedative might take a few hours to wear off so after you leave here, take him home and let him sleep.'

'Uh…oh. All right, then.' Tan stood by, nervously watching as the two doctors worked together. Clover sat Ryder up as Brandon sprayed midazolam into Ryder's nose, knowing it wouldn't take long for the medication to be absorbed and cause him to become drowsy.

'If you could just tilt him—' No sooner were the words out of Brandon's mouth than Clover had Ryder in the correct position with his head on the side, ear up. 'Er…thanks.' Brandon pulled the lamp attached to an articulating arm towards Ryder so he could see more clearly.

'He's ready,' Clover announced, ensuring she had a steady grip on the boy. It took the work of a moment for Brandon to reach in with the forceps and extract the offending article. He held it to the light and all of the adults peered closer to see what it was.

'It's a miniature car!'

'How on earth…?' Tan stared at it in astonishment. 'I have no idea where that came from.'

Clover smiled as Brandon dropped the car into the kidney dish and took another look in Ryder's ear to ensure there was no damage. 'Kids pick things up from all sorts of places. Friends' houses, playgroups. It's quite easy so don't go beating yourself up about it. You acted promptly to his crying, brought him in here, and as Brandon is now packing everything up, we can clearly deduce that there will be no long-lasting effects to this incident.'

'The ear canal does looks fine,' Brandon added, confirming Clover's words. 'A little red from having a foreign object shoved down it so I'll give you a prescription for antibiotics just to be on the safe side.'

'And he won't have any pain or anything?' Tan was looking at her son, rubbing her hand over his head as he lay dozing in Clover's arms.

'He'll be as right as rain by tonight,' Clover promised, smiling brightly at the caring mother. 'You're doing a wonderful job.'

Brandon watched as Tan smiled shyly at Clover's praise.

'Let me carry him out to the car for you.' Clover stood, ensured Tan had the prescription and waited while Brandon opened the consulting-room door for them.

'Thank you,' she said, and headed out with Tan.

Brandon watched them go, shaking his head slowly. What was it about Clover Farraday that seemed to mesmerise anyone she came into contact with? Even at the wedding he'd noticed the way men looked at her, at the way women seemed to respond naturally to her smile. When they'd been dancing, talking about the maternity centre, when he'd stood in the middle of the street and waved her goodbye, Brandon had felt a connection. He'd felt important, felt as though he and his opinions mattered. He'd seen the same sort of look cross Tan's face before she'd followed Clover out of the clinic.

Perhaps it was Clover's heartfelt words, or the way she looked directly at you, giving you her undivided attention, that caused the sensation. Either way, Brandon could tell she had a true gift when it came to the patients of the Goldmark Family Medical Practice and surely that was all that mattered, right?

It did leave him wondering whether the attraction, the connection he felt towards Clover, was merely the result of her natural attention or whether he was once again falling victim to a smooth-talking woman who would break his heart with her lies and deception. Was Clover for real? Could she honestly be trusted? Brandon frowned as the thoughts continued to whirl around his mind, finally deciding that it was up to him to find out.

By the end of most days, Clover had to admit she was exhausted. She'd never been as happy in her life but still she was very tired. The small community, even though it covered a vast area, was extremely tight-knit and everyone knew everyone, which meant everyone knew everyone else's business. Gossip was rampant and every patient who came into the clinic to see her would spend an extra ten minutes just wanting to talk, to share, to involve Clover in their lives.

After two weeks in Lewisville, she now knew that Susie Moffat was the 'go-to' woman in the community if she wanted any sort of knitting or crocheting pattern. Marissa Mandocicelli was a brilliant cook. May Finnegan collected every recipe she could get her hands on and Andie Davis was the best quilter in the district.

All of them held Viola, Brandon and Ruby in high esteem and a few of the young women who came to see her had once been runaway or difficult teens, having stayed with Viola years ago and with her help and guidance had managed to turn their lives around.

'It must be so rewarding to see these women, who were once hurt and conflicted, living happy and healthy lives,' Clover remarked to Viola that evening as she helped prepare the evening meal. After Clover's first week there, Viola had been horrified to learn Clover didn't cook much and had made it her mission to teach Clover as much as she could.

'It's very rewarding.' Viola nodded, a bright light shining in her eyes. 'I expect you feel that same sort of feeling when you help one of your patients.'

'I guess so.' Clover's brow was puckered in a frown as she concentrated on her task. Viola looked down at the chopping board and praised Clover's efforts.

'Excellent chopping of the garnish. Nice and small. Now stir the sauce while I check the chicken in the oven,' Viola said as she removed the baking dish from the oven and took off the foil lid. 'See how the chicken looks? When it gets to this stage, you know it's time to add the sauce and then all those delicious flavours will infuse and...' Viola brought her fingers to her mouth and made a kissing noise.

The delicious aromas were starting to make Clover realise just how hungry she was and she wasn't surprised when her stomach grumbled. She'd come home from the clinic and been ordered by Viola to shower and freshen up. When that had been done, it had been time for her next cooking lesson. Clover poured the sauce over the chicken pieces before Viola put the foil back on and placed the dish back in the oven.

'It's just as well the maternity centre is up and running because I've been so worried about Brandon.'

'Brandon? Why?'

'These last four or five months it's as though he's been pushing himself too hard. Running on empty. I don't want him to work himself into an early grave.'

Clover swallowed over the sudden dryness of her throat at Viola's words. Even the fleeting thought of something happening to Brandon made her feel ill. 'We don't want that.'

'No.' Viola closed the oven and straightened up.

'Hopefully now I'm here, it'll take some of the pressure off.'

'You've taken a lot of pressure off him. Setting up the programmes and helping the women to know they're not alone has been a huge weight lifted from his shoulders, plus helping in the clinic while Ruby and Hamilton are away also helps.' Viola sighed. 'I just wish you could stay longer.'

'You mean after my three months?'

'Exactly. Even with Ruby and Hamilton back

in Lewisville, the maternity centre will still require an OB/GYN to run it. What do you think about staying on?'

'That's a good question,' Brandon commented as he sauntered into the kitchen. He crossed to the bench and stole a piece of carrot from the dish, neatly shifting out of the way before his mother smacked his hand.

'Leave the dinner alone. Cheeky boy,' Viola chided, but Brandon only winked at his mother and munched on the carrot stick.

'Smells great.'

'Good. Clover's been learning how to cook.'

'You don't know how to cook?' Brandon was surprised by that and it only reiterated just how little he knew about his beautiful colleague.

Clover's answer was a shrug of her shoulders. 'Your mother's a great teacher.'

'Thank you, Clover, but you're avoiding the question. What are your plans once you leave Lewisville?'

Clover looked from Brandon to Viola and back again, realising she had the full attention of both Goldmarks. 'Well...before I left to come here, the CEO of the hospital I work at was eager for me to develop more maternity programmes so I'll be off to train staff at Walgett in upper New South Wales, where they're planning on opening a centre.'

'I see.' Brandon exhaled slowly. 'I guess the maternity centres really are your baby, given you were the one to develop the programmes in the first place.'

'Well, yes, but—'

'You're doing good work,' Viola added. 'We can't fault that, can we, Brandon?'

'But I do like—'

'Can't fault it.' Brandon nodded. 'It's good to know. Means I can try and advertise for another OB/GYN to come here once you leave.'

'It won't be easy. Not many specialists want to come to the Outback,' Viola agreed.

'Especially on a permanent basis.' Brandon took another carrot but this time Viola didn't even attempt to slap his hand. They both seemed despondent and Clover wanted to agree right then and there that she would love nothing better than to stay in Lewisville for the rest of her life and run the little maternity centre.

At both the Blue Mountains and Tathra clinics, she'd not only adjusted the programmes but she'd trained the staff, which was what she'd be doing in Walgett. Then after Walgett, there would probably be another clinic and more adjusting and training and…

Was that what she really wanted? There were a few other specialists at the Blue Mountain clinic who were more than capable of training the staff at Walgett. Here in Lewisville there was no other specialist but her. If she left and Brandon was unable to secure the services of another specialist, what would happen to the women of this community?

Plus there was also her father to consider. She might have been annoyed with him, desperate for him to realise she and Xavier were incompatible when she'd left to come here, but at the end of the day he *was* her father. She was an only child. She'd lost her mother and now the only real family she had left was her dad and despite their strange relationship, she wasn't sure she could move out here permanently without some sort of acknowledgement from him.

Xavier, well, hopefully if she did move to Lewisville permanently, it would slowly sink into his very thick skull that she wasn't going to marry him.

And that left Brandon. She swallowed as she looked at him, munching on another carrot as Viola finished off the dinner preparations. Would she be able to work alongside Brandon day in, day out and control the rising attraction she felt for him?

If she stayed, was it a possibility they might actually be able to figure out exactly what their relationship was? Would it be more than just colleagues? Was it worth the sacrifice of resigning from her job at St. Aloysius, giving up her connection to the working model of the maternity care centre and moving permanently here in the hope that it might happen?

Her heart rate increased at the thought of herself and Brandon together, laughing as they walked down the street holding hands, building a billy-cart together, helping their patients before going home to their own place in the evenings, content to simply *be* with each other.

Brandon's mobile phone rang, cutting into her thoughts, and he swallowed his mouthful before answering it. 'Brandon Goldmark,' he said into the phone, then a second later, 'Lacey? Calm down. Yes, yes. She's right here.' He held out the phone to Clover.

'Lacey Millar. Thinks she might be in labour.'

'Right.' Clover accepted the phone. 'Hi, Lacey. Have you been having some pain?'

Brandon marvelled at the way her tone was smooth and calm and completely in control. It was the same tone she'd used on the helicopter when she'd been talking to Suzanne, or when she'd been talking to Ryder's mother, or talking with any of her patients. Calm and in control.

'All right,' she was saying. 'I want you to lie down. Find a position that's the most comfortable and see if Damien can massage your back for you. Just concentrate on breathing nice and calmly. Brandon and I will come immediately so we'll be there in ten—'

'Fifteen,' Brandon quickly corrected her.

'Fifteen minutes,' she said. 'All right. Just relax. We'll see you soon. Bye.' Clover pressed the button to end the call and handed the phone back to Brandon, their fingers touching briefly in the exchange. She tried not to gasp as a wave of glorious warmth spread up her arm and exploded throughout the rest of her body.

'Uh…Viola?'

'I know. I'll dish up a plate of food for you both and put it in the fridge for whenever you get back.'

'Do you want to move Lacey to the maternity centre? Should I contact Joan?' Brandon asked, but Clover shook her head.

'Lacey's not in labour. This is a false alarm.'

'How can you tell?' he asked, completely perplexed.

'Because I'm clever.' She smiled. 'And because I've delivered well in excess of a hundred babies. My record was four in one day, all single babies from four different mothers,' she pointed out. 'I can tell by the way Lacey was breathing, by the tone of her voice.'

'Then why are we going to her place?'

'To reassure her. She may not go into labour for another few days—a week or two at best—and in the meantime the more sleep she can get, the more relaxed she is, the better it will all be when it comes to crunch time.'

'Fair enough.' He pulled his keys from his pocket. 'Shall we?'

Clover's smile increased. 'Just let me get my bag.' She headed into her room, noticing a lightness to her step, and she knew it had nothing to do with going to check on Lacey Millar and everything to do with spending one-on-one time with her handsome colleague.

CHAPTER EIGHT

DURING the fifteen-minute drive to the Millar house, which was situated just outside the main town of Lewisville, Brandon asked Clover about some of the baby deliveries she'd performed over the years. It was clear she was more than happy to talk about that side of her past and hopefully it would help her to relax a bit more and perhaps he could ask her more about her family and her life in Sydney.

He'd caught a glimpse of her face when he'd been talking about advertising for another specialist to come to Lewisville when her three months was up and he'd been surprised at the thoughtful look in her eyes. Was it possible she might actually decide to stay here in Lewisville? To continue running the maternity centre on a full-time basis?

On a professional level, he wanted that to happen more than anything simply because Clover was one of the best doctors he'd worked alongside. On a personal level, he had no idea how he'd be able to cope with fighting the constant attraction he felt for her.

Even here, within the close confines of the car, he was having to force himself to concentrate on driving rather than on the lovely lilt of her voice as she recounted a story of delivering a baby in a hotel restroom.

'The poor woman was mortified when she realised she hadn't *really* needed to go to the toilet. So there we both were, dressed up to the nines, in the ladies' restroom, her pushing and screaming abuse at her husband, who flatly refused to come in as it was *the ladies' room*, and me using whatever first-aid equipment the hotel had in order to bring bub safely into the world.'

'And the ambulance?'

'It arrived twenty minutes after the event.'

'Of course.'

Clover shrugged. 'There's a lot of traffic in Sydney. They do their best.'

'And I'll bet once mother, baby and father were

on their way to the hospital, you simply washed your hands and returned to the hotel function?'

She smiled. 'No. Thanks to the delivery, I managed to wangle my way out of having to go back and sit in a ballroom full of people I don't know, listening to my father make a speech about how brilliant he is.'

'Why were you there in the first place?'

'Because he asked me to go…and, well, my dad doesn't ask me to do a lot of things with him, so when he does, I usually say yes.'

Brandon nodded. 'I think when you lose one parent, you really hang on to the other for dear life.'

'Yes. Exactly. Well, of course you'd understand. It's clear from the way both you and your mother talk about your dad that you were all very close.' Clover sighed. 'That's nice. Precious.'

Brandon slowed the car and turned off the dirt road onto a thin dirt driveway that led to the Millars' farmhouse. He didn't want this ride to end, especially as Clover hadn't clammed up at all. Perhaps now that she was getting to know him better, she'd be more forthcoming. He could only hope that was the case because he *really* was interested in *her*. Initially, he'd wanted to make sure she wasn't pulling the wool over his eyes, or the eyes of the community at large, but now he simply wanted to know more because she'd proved to be a person worth knowing.

Damien Millar was out on the front porch, running down to meet them the instant he spotted Brandon's vehicle. 'Thanks for coming. She's inside. I think she's resting. I tried rubbing her back, like you said, Clover, but in the end she said it made her even more uncomfortable.'

'Not to worry, Damien,' Clover replied as she carried her medical bag and followed the two men inside. 'At this stage, it's better to let Lacey call the shots.' She was led into the main bedroom, where she was astonished to find Lacey lying flat on her back with her legs going up the wall.

A smile sprang to her lips. 'Seriously? That's a comfortable position?' she asked on a laugh as she knelt down beside Lacey, her tone light and free.

'Is it wrong? Will it hurt the baby?'

'You're fine, Lacey, but I might get you to just shift a little and put your legs back on the floor so I can examine you.' She opened her bag and took out her portable sphygmomanometer, taking Lacey's blood pressure and declaring everything was nice and normal.

'The pains have stopped,' Lacey confessed. 'And now I feel guilty for asking you to come all the way out here. I was going to get Damien to call you and tell you not to bother but I really wanted you to come and just…'

'Reassure you? It's no trouble, Lacey. This is what I'm here for. To help you through this time, to guide you, to answer your questions, no matter how silly you might think they are.'

'Do I need to go to the maternity centre?'

'Not just yet. You've had what we call a false labour and right now everything is back to normal. You're fine to stay home, to do everything you usually do.'

'But it *is* starting to happen, right? I *am* going to go into labour soon?'

'Things are progressing but it might be as long as another two weeks before you actually go into labour, Lacey.' Clover brushed some hair out of the woman's forehead and again Brandon was struck by the way she *really* cared for her patients.

'But what if things go like this again and I get more contractions? Or my waters break?'

'Then you call me and I'll come running.'

'But I don't want to bother you or—'

'Shh,' she crooned. 'Lacey. I'm here for *you*. We'll work it out together. You, me, Damien, Brandon. We're all in this together. There's an old joke I remember my mother telling me. 'How do you eat an elephant?'

Lacey looked at her and shook her head.

'One bite at a time,' Clover answered. 'The point is to just relax. Try, as hard as it might be, to enjoy your time with just you and Damien because once this baby's born, things will be different for ever.'

Lacey nodded, clearly much calmer, and after helping her up from the floor they all had a soothing cup of herbal tea before Brandon and Clover took their leave, heading back to Lewisville, both content to listen and sing along to a Christmas CD.

'I've never sung along with someone else in the car before,' she remarked as he parked the car and the two of them alighted. Clover carried her medical bag with her as they walked to the foot of the steps outside Viola's house. It was exactly where they'd been standing on her first night in town after they'd returned from taking the teenagers to Broken Hill hospital. 'It was fun.'

'It *was* fun,' he agreed, and took her medical bag from her hands, putting it on the step out of the way. Tonight, watching her with Lacey, wondering what life would be like in Lewisville after Clover left, Brandon had realised one very important thing. Clover belonged here. In Lewisville. Working alongside him. It was a strange revelation and one that had completely stunned him. Now, though, he was unsure what to do next, how to proceed with this new-found information.

'Don't you sometimes wish life could be as fun as it was when you were a kid?'

'Not really. As previously stated...' she pointed to herself '...not a happy childhood.'

'Sorry. Momentarily forgot.' He thought for a second. 'OK, name one memory where you felt completely happy. I mean giddily happy. So happy with carefree freedom that you honestly thought you were going to burst. The crazy, silly, happy type of happy.'

He watched as a slow smile crossed Clover's face and after a brief pause she said, 'Dancing.'

'Dancing? Did your mother take you dancing?'

'No. I meant here.' She pointed down the road. 'At your sister's wedding. With you.'

Brandon was stunned, his heart pierced with surprise and sadness. 'Your one complete and utter moment of crazy, silly, happiness was when you were dancing at my sister's wedding?'

'With you.'

He looked more intently at her, wondering if she was pulling his leg, but from what she'd just told him about her life, it appeared she was indeed telling the truth. Poor Clover. To have been raised with such an uncaring and indifferent father. He found it difficult to imagine as his own dad had been so opposite.

Now, though, Brandon had the opportunity to provide her with a moment of happiness and, given what she'd shared, he was going to do just that. He stepped back and formally bowed before holding out his arms to her.

'May I have this dance?'

Clover frowned, a little confused. Had he just asked her to dance? 'Pardon?'

'Would you like to dance?'

'But there's no music.'

'Do you *need* music?'

Clover tilted her head to the side for a moment and considered the question. 'I guess not.' Her hair was heavy and tangled and she quickly pulled it from the band, letting it fall loose around her shoulders. If she was going to enjoy crazy, silly happiness with Brandon, dancing with him in the moonlight, then she was going to be comfortable.

Brandon had been about to speak but at her actions felt as though he'd just swallowed his tongue. Good heavens! Didn't the woman have any idea how alluring she was? He cleared his throat, standing in the street outside his mother's house, arms out wide, waiting for her. 'Well, then…surely you're not going to leave me standing here, are you?'

'No.' She raised her arms and slipped her hands into his. The moment they touched, Brandon started shuffling his feet, swaying from side to side. Clover couldn't help the giggle that bubbled up from deep inside.

'Something wrong, Dr Farraday?'

'No, there is not, Dr Goldmark. Except for the fact that I'm dancing in the middle of the road, in the Outback, with no music.'

'And you're having fun!'

'I'm having crazy, silly, happy fun,' she confirmed as he twirled them round. She laughed and looked up into his eyes. Even though it was dark, the moon in the sky was shining enough for her to see his face. There was no doubt about the attraction that existed between them and there was no doubt they were both feeling the same things but due to past hurts, past circumstances, neither were exactly sure how best to proceed.

They continued to move, shifting gently from side to side, Brandon's steps nowhere near as long as they'd been a few moments ago. He looked into her eyes, the warmth of his body close, his fresh scent winding its way through her senses, drawing her in, hypnotising her, making her desperate to take huge steps away from the secure walls she'd spent a long time erecting.

Was it time to slowly let them down? To let Brandon into her life? Would he hurt her? Would he accept her for who she was? Could she confess she'd come to Lewisville because she hadn't been able to stop thinking about him? Could she tell him who her father was? Could she trust him with the truth? Would it change the way he was presently looking at her? How *did* he feel about her? Perhaps she should just come right out and ask him…but in a roundabout way, of course.

'Brandon…'

'Clover.' He spoke her name as though it were the most perfect caress ever to leave his lips.

'Do you remember my first night here?'

'Yes.'

'When we were walking back from the helicopter and you were talking about Lynn, about how she'd hurt you?'

'Mmm-hmm.'

'I made a comment that she'd broken your heart and you said—'

'I thought she'd broken it,' he interrupted.

'But you weren't so sure. What does that mean?'

'Are you sure you want to know?'

'Yes.'

'It means I want to kiss you. It means that I've *wanted* to kiss you ever since your first night here. It means that if my mother hadn't interrupted us with an emergency, I may well have followed through on that urge and kissed you, Clover.' He looked up at the porch swing. 'Right up there.'

Her lips parted and she stared up at him in stunned disbelief.

'I haven't wanted to kiss any other woman since Lynn. You're the first.' He let go of her hand and tenderly reached out to scoop up a small handful of her hair.

'Just like I've always wanted to touch your hair, ever since my sister's wedding, to feel it slip through my fingers, so soft and silky.' He swallowed and she watched his Adam's apple slide up and down his throat. 'I'm not sure if you even realise just how alluring you are, driving me to distraction every time I see you.'

'Uh…um…' She bit her lip.

'And the way you bite your lip or tuck your hair behind your ear.' He did just that and tucked a lock behind one ear, then slid his hand around her waist, drawing her even closer.

'Oh.' Her gaze flicked between his mouth as he spoke and his mesmerising blue eyes. She sighed, feeling much more than just crazy, silly, happy. She felt *free*. Completely and utterly free, and she couldn't ever remember feeling this way before.

'You…set me on fire when you say things like that.' Her breathing had increased and she slipped her tongue out to wet her suddenly dry lips. Brandon's gaze dipped to her mouth, following the action quite intently.

'Good.' He angled his head down, just a touch, bringing them a little closer than before.

'I don't know if it's good or bad or crazy-silly.'

'You forgot happy.'

Clover slid her hands from his shoulders down to rest on his chest, delighting in the firmness beneath his T-shirt, amazed at being able to touch him and fulfil one of the fantasies she'd often dreamed about. This really was crazy-silly, this powerful, magnetic attraction drawing them closer and closer together.

He was looking at her mouth now and she felt the fire inside ignite the next round of flames. Although she wanted nothing more than to kiss him, there was still something holding her back and she knew what it was. The plain and simple truth was that Brandon didn't like liars and here she was, standing in his arms, unable to find the words to tell him the truth of her situation. What if she told him who her father was and he rejected her? She wasn't sure she'd cope.

Biting her lip again, she eased slightly back and met his gaze. 'Brandon. My life is…not as straightforward as other people's lives.'

'Mmm-hmm.' Brandon nodded and she wondered if he was really listening.

'It's a little confusing at times and what with my father and—'

'Mmm?' he murmured again. 'I don't want to talk about your father, or anyone else for that matter. I want to dance with you in the moonlight, to forget the world, to stop the turning of the clock and just *be* in this moment.'

'But that's what I'm trying to— Oh, my!' She gasped as he brushed her hair to the side and dipped his head, pressing small butterfly kisses to her neck. Clover closed her eyes and tilted her head to the side, granting him access.

'But that's…the…point. My fath…' She was having a difficult time thinking, forming complete and coherent sentences, especially with the way he was now nuzzling her neck. The warm breath and the soft touch of his lips on her skin caused goose-bumps to spread like wildfire up and down her spine.

'What *is* the point?' he whispered near her ear, before pressing little kisses along her jaw.

'The point is…' She swallowed and parted her lips, her breathing almost out of control as he continued to make his way around towards her mouth. *Brandon is going to kiss you!* The words seemed to be screaming through her mind like an adolescent teenager high on excitement.

She'd dreamt of this moment over and over since the night of Ruby and Hamilton's wedding, which was the last time they'd danced together. Of course, she hadn't exactly pictured their first kiss to be quite like this, standing outside his mother's house, Christmas lights twinkling around them, making the street look like a magical fairyland and dancing with no music, but she wasn't about to quibble.

The fact of the matter was that Brandon was slowly and tenderly working his way towards her mouth, his eagerness and determination quite clear in their objective.

'I don't *know* what the point is,' she whispered, her words breathless, her mind unable to think clearly due to the havoc he was creating with her senses.

'Good, because I've been waiting to do this for far too long,' he returned, and before she could say anything else he'd covered her mouth with his, causing her to gasp with longing and delight.

The kiss was brief, testing, and he slowly pulled

back—just a fraction—in order to try and gauge her reaction. Her eyes remained closed, her face upturned towards him, and as he gazed down at her lovely features, her straight nose, her parted lips, her dark lashes, he swallowed, unable to believe how incredibly perfect this woman was.

How could any man not cherish her? How could any man not be completely smitten by her and her incredible features? How could he stand here, with her leaning towards him and not plunder her mouth with all the fire, hunger and passion that was coursing through him at this very moment?

He shook his head, the movement barely perceptible but he knew the last thing she needed right now was to have the extent of his powerful need unleashed when instead she should be handled carefully and tenderly. She deserved it.

Slowly, he removed his hands from her waist and brought them to her face, sliding his fingers gently across her lower jaw, cupping her face and tilting her head upwards. As he continued to look at her, seeing the total trust, expectation and intrigue in her features, he knew what he felt for her wasn't a ploy or an innocent seduction.

Didn't she have any idea just how powerfully she affected him?

Brandon lowered his head and pressed soft and tender kisses to first one closed eyelid then the other, secretly pleased when she gasped with surprised delight, her mouth opening a little wider. It was difficult for him to restrain himself when she behaved in such an adorable and innocent manner, but when his lips finally made contact with hers once more, he kept a tight leash on the hunger that now burned through him.

One, two, three more tiny, tantalising kisses before Clover leaned forward and pressed her open mouth to his, determined to deepen the kiss and have her fill of the man who was driving her to utter distraction. Didn't he have any idea how powerfully he affected her? She wanted him to know that whatever was happening between them was most definitely not one-sided.

'Clover?' Her name was a caress upon his lips. 'Is this what you want?'

'Shh,' she whispered, and urged his head down, the raging fire and burning desperation she'd been trying to deny since they'd first met bursting forth and overflowing.

She could tell he thought she was a tender little flower who no doubt needed to be treated with kid gloves, but he was wrong. She was a woman, a passionate woman, a woman who was more than happy to share in such an intimate, fiery moment with him and unleash her hunger for him.

The instant she deepened the kiss, he stilled, just for a split second as though his mind was working out what was happening, before hauling her as close as he possibly could, their bodies pressed firmly against each other as they gave way to the repressed sensations that both had pushed aside for what seemed like an eternity.

Never had he felt so drugged, so helpless, so desperate as he did holding Clover in his arms, his mouth moving over hers with such a sense of urgency, a sense she appeared to match in every way, shape and form.

Until this moment, with her summery scent winding its way about him, drugging his senses to where he couldn't focus on anything but her, he'd had no idea she'd felt the same irrepressible tug, the one that appeared to have been drawing them together since they'd first met. He'd tried to fight it and now, understanding her need as it mirrored his own, he realised he'd been a fool right from the start.

With Clover in his arms, her body against his, her mouth seeking, demanding and finding a response to the delight flowing between them, Brandon could well believe that *anything* in life was possible. He could also now admit that what he'd thought he'd felt for Lynn had been nothing compared to the wildfire blazing through him as he readily accepted everything the angel in his arms had to give, while giving to her in return.

Equality. Both had taken the plunge, had stepped out onto a quivering ledge of uncertainty and together had discovered a raging, mutual passion.

Clover was amazed at the intensity but pleased it wasn't one-sided. It didn't even seem to matter that her lungs felt as though they would burst if she didn't drag oxygen into them, simply because she couldn't bear the thought of not having Brandon's mouth on her own.

When he eased back slightly, his arms still firmly wrapped around her body, she was pleased to note his breathing was as erratic as hers.

He kissed her again and again, as though unable to stop himself, needing to reassure himself that this was really happening. Slowly the pressure in her lungs began to ease as her breathing returned to normal. She spread butterfly kisses across his jaw, her lips tingling from his whiskers as he no doubt hadn't shaved since that morning.

At his throat, she continued to kiss his skin, pressing a soft kiss to his Adam's apple, her body still close as she stopped standing on tiptoe and rested her head against his chest.

Sighing with a happiness she'd never known she could feel, Clover was pleased to note his heart rate was as wild as her own. He began to sway again and she shuffled her feet beside his as they moved in unison.

'Do you hear that music?' he murmured. 'I've never heard it before but when I'm with you, it plays so clearly inside my head.'

Clover smiled against his chest. 'It's beautiful music.'

'Soft.'

'Intimate.'

'The perfect beat.'

'It matches our hearts.'

Brandon chuckled at her words and eased back a little, causing Clover to lift her head and look up into his face. 'That's a corny line.'

She shrugged a shoulder. 'What's wrong with being corny?'

He chuckled again and shook his head. 'Nothing. Nothing at all.' He brushed a soft kiss across her lips. 'This isn't normal, Clover.'

'I know.'

'I don't mean me kissing someone…or even me kissing you. I mean the kisses we just *shared*. That sort of thing doesn't—'

She reached up and kissed him, effectively shutting him up. 'Shh. I know.' And as he looked down into her upturned face, he realised she *did* know, that what had just transpired between them was something new, something different, something unique.

'You've never felt this way with anyone—' He found he couldn't even finish the sentence as the thought of Clover kissing any other man filled him with a possessive jealousy.

'No.' Her reply was instant.

'Do you…date much?'

She glanced away for a moment not really wanting to mention Xavier or the way he treated her like some sort of commodity. 'I'm a busy doctor, delivering babies at all hours of the day and night.'

'There's no one important in your life?' He shook his head, unable to believe how incredible she could make him feel. After Lynn, he'd thought he'd never experience such a powerful, possessive need ever again and yet she always seemed so evasive when he mentioned her life in Sydney. 'I feel like I know nothing about you, about your life in Sydney.'

'It's irrelevant because when I'm with you I feel more alive than ever before.'

From what she'd said about her father and her lonely childhood, he hoped it was the truth. Lynn had said something similar to him in the beginning and look how that had turned out. 'Really?'

She looked into his eyes, her words intent. 'One

hundred per cent. The woman I am with you is not the woman I am with everyone else. Around you...I can be...' She shrugged one elegant shoulder. 'I can be *me*. The *real* me.'

'How are you with everyone else?'

She sighed. 'Meek. Oppressed. Sad.' She raked her fingers through his hair, loving the way she could touch him without having to figure out some sort of excuse to be close. 'Lewisville makes me happy.' She smiled shyly at him. '*You* make me happy, Brandon.'

He nodded slowly as he looked down into the chocolaty-brown depths of her eyes. 'What do you think we should do about this attraction?'

'We don't ignore it, that's for sure.'

Brandon exhaled and nodded. 'Agreed.' He smiled as he met her gaze. 'How could anyone possibly ignore you?'

'More easily than you would think.' Clover let out a deep sigh.

'You really haven't had a happy life, have you,' he stated rhetorically.

'As I've said before, it was a...different life from most.' When he started to ask her another question, Clover leaned up and pressed her mouth to his once more, effectively silencing him in the best way possible. She didn't want to talk about her past, about her life, because up until she'd first come to Lewisville her life had consisted of being in a holding pattern.

It was as though she'd been waiting for this, waiting for Brandon for the past thirty-one years, and when she was with him, feeling his arms holding her close, his mouth moving over hers as though they'd been designed for each other, it was all she could do not to sigh and wish upon a star that this could be her life for ever.

She knew she had to tell him about her father, about her Sydney life and the way Xavier didn't seem able to take 'no' for an answer, but this life here in Lewisville was so glorious she wanted it to last for a bit longer before the reality came crashing down on them.

'We have work tomorrow,' he murmured against her mouth as she slowly drew away.

'Patients who need us.'

'The price of responsibility.' He shook his head. 'Why is it our bodies require sleep?'

Clover smiled and brushed a kiss across his lips before easing out of the embrace but continued to hold on to his hand as she bent to pick up her bag. He walked with her, up the steps, and the porch security light came on, causing them both to squint. Brandon pressed one last kiss to her lips then with great reluctance let her go. 'Dream of me.'

'It would be difficult not to.' With a sigh she turned and headed into the house, ensuring the screen door didn't bang lest she should wake Viola, which was the last thing she wanted right now. How to explain to Viola that she was fast falling in love with her son was a conversation Clover wasn't ready to have...just yet.

She breezed through her night-time routine then snuggled into the pillows, hugging one close, pretending it was Brandon. Then with a goofy smile on her face she drifted off into one of the loveliest sleeps she had in such a very long time and it was all because Brandon had kissed her... *really* kissed her.

CHAPTER NINE

THAT morning, Clover almost danced her way through the clinic, feeling as though she was walking on feathers or pillows on air. At breakfast, Viola had laughed at her when she'd waltzed into the kitchen and placed a kiss on Viola's cheek.

'You've woken up in a good mood,' Viola said.

'The absolute best,' Clover admitted, accepting a glass of freshly squeezed orange juice. When she arrived at the clinic, Joan was astonished as Lewisville's OB/GYN danced in through the door, a big smile beaming on her face.

'Cup of tea?' Clover asked, and at Joan's bemused nod Clover headed to the kitchenette. Brandon wasn't in yet, which surprised her, but when he did arrive, rushing in ten minutes late, he found her still in the kitchenette. He stopped in the doorway and stared at her, their gazes holding, both of them uncertain for one split second, unsure what was supposed to happen next.

It didn't take Brandon long to decide and within a moment he crossed to her side and crushed her to him in a firm but powerful kiss.

'I overslept,' he told her as he drank her in. Her hair was pulled back into a perfect bun on top of her head, her cream-coloured shirt and pale green pencil-thin skirt highlighting her slim waist and gorgeous curves. 'You're a sight for sore eyes.'

Clover smiled at his words, unable to believe how shy she felt when he said such things. She simply wasn't used to compliments, especially from a man who was coming to mean so much to her. 'Tea?'

'I think I need coffee this morning. Have to get my mind back into gear, rather than allowing it to stay in Clover-land.'

A buzz of excitement rippled through her. 'Clover-land?'

He winked at her and smiled but didn't elaborate any further. As they made hot drinks, brushing up against each other and shamelessly flirting, she couldn't believe how happy he made her feel.

'From the look of the patient lists this morning, we should be done by about two o'clock, then we can get started on the billy-cart…uh, if that's all right with you.'

'I'd forgotten about the billy-cart.'

He raised an eyebrow. 'You do still want to do it, don't you?'

'Yes. Yes, of course.' Clover headed out of the kitchenette, two cups in her hand, but stopped for a moment and looked at him over her shoulder. 'See you later.' And then she did something she'd never done before. She returned his wink and swished her hips as she walked away. Her reward was an audible groan of agonised delight.

By three o'clock they were in his mother's shed, hammering and building, Clover more than happy to follow Brandon's instructions on what he needed her to do.

'You've really never built anything before?'

'Never.'

'Not even put together a piece of furniture? A bookshelf?'

Clover shook her head. 'No.'

'But you do have furniture in your...apartment? I presume you have an apartment in Sydney?' He shook his head. 'There is just so much I don't know about you.'

Clover smiled and touched a hand to his cheek. 'I have an apartment.' But she didn't add that it was on the prestigious North Shore and overlooked the Opera House and Sydney Harbour Bridge. 'It came furnished.'

When she'd decided to move out of her father's mansion, without asking, he'd organised her apartment with everything provided. She'd thought it might have been a small token of his affection, to reward her for becoming an obstetric consultant, but when she'd made the effort to thank him, he'd told her it was business, that he'd recently purchased the entire apartment complex and would receive a hefty tax break.

She pushed aside thoughts of her father and held up the hammer. 'What do I need to bash in next?'

Brandon tut-tutted. 'You don't *bash*, Clover, you gently tap the nail at first and then, once the tip is in the wood, you add a bit more oomph.'

'Oomph?' She smiled at the word. 'Is that the technical term? And why are you allowed to say the word "oomph" when I'm not allowed to say "bash"?'

Brandon laughed and hugged her close. 'I've never had this much fun building a billy-cart before.'

'Not even with your dad?'

'No. He was too big and hairy to kiss.'

Clover laughed at his words, slipping her hands around his waist and angling her head up so he could give her another one of the amazing kisses she was quickly become addicted to.

'You're much nicer,' he murmured against her mouth. 'Delicious. Addictive.' He punctuated his words with kisses and Clover sighed into him.

He closed his eyes and gave himself over to her glorious lips and the way she responded to him so ardently. Did it matter that she was still a little closed off with him? That each time he mentioned he didn't know her all that well, she'd offer him the slightest bit of information and then change the subject?

He could sense she was keeping something

from him but right now, with her arms wrapped firmly around him, returning his kisses with such an ardent passion, he wasn't too sure he wanted to find out.

For the rest of the week they worked alongside each other at the clinic and maternity care centre, looking after their patients and providing top-of-the-line health care for the township and surrounding district. After work, enjoying the extended daylight hours, they'd hammer and build and laugh together out in the shed. Many other people were building their own billy-carts and on Friday night, their entry finally ready for tomorrow's big Christmas race, Clover and Brandon headed to the pub for a well-deserved drink.

'You've got paint on your cheek,' Brandon remarked as they sat down at a table, gently rubbing his thumb over the mark, his touch sweet and tender. Clover smiled as she sipped her ice-cold orange juice.

'How do I look in green paint?' she asked, leaning closer to his ear to deliver her words as the crowd behind them was starting to get a bit rowdy.

'Stunning,' he returned, his gaze devouring her. Throughout the week they'd tried to play down their new relationship, both of them still finding their feet, but that hadn't stopped the gossipers from doing what they did best.

'Mind if we join you?' Geoffrey asked, as he and Joan came to sit at the table. 'It's getting a tad crowded at the bar,' he remarked, jerking a thumb over his shoulder.

'Of course.' Clover and Brandon sat back in their chairs, smiling as though they shared an incredible secret. As they chatted to their friends, discussing an emergency plan for tomorrow's race should it be required, Brandon couldn't believe how content he felt with Clover by his side. The wariness he'd lived with since discovering Lynn's betrayal had all but vanished and he was glad he'd taken a chance with Clover as he was falling for her in a big way.

He'd learned over the past few days that Clover's favourite colour was green—hence their billy-cart was predominantly painted green, with two thin red racing stripes down the sides. 'To make it go faster,' Brandon had answered when Clover had queried it.

He'd learned she had a bit of a sweet tooth and would often take a smaller portion of the main meal if there was dessert being served afterwards. He'd learned she wasn't afraid to try something new when she'd joined the Lewisville quilters, even though she'd confessed to never having sewn before.

'Except for suturing wounds closed,' she'd added when he'd looked at her askance.

He'd learned she hadn't obtained her driver's licence until after her twenty-third birthday, saying she'd lived close to the medical school where she'd completed her training so hadn't really needed to drive.

But most of all he'd learned that she'd 'sort of dated' a younger colleague of her father's until a few months ago.

'We were a wrong fit right from the start,' she'd ventured as they'd sanded back the billy-cart before applying the first coat of paint. 'My father likes him and therefore approves but unlike my sanding, which is perfectly smooth, our time together was anything but that.'

'Then why date him in the first place?'

'Because my father approved.' She'd frowned. 'Sad but true.'

'You want his attention. I understand that.'

'I don't know if I'm ever going to get it.' She'd shaken her head and sighed. 'Since coming here, seeing a way of life that's so completely different from my own, I'm realising I need to stop looking for his approval. You've taught me that.'

'I have?'

'Sure. You accept me for who I am and you have no idea how…empowering that is.'

Brandon had felt a little uncomfortable with her words because he knew, in the beginning, he *hadn't*. He'd been hurt and bruised and highly sceptical but being here with her, getting to know her, having her finally open up and trust him a little bit more, had made him realise just how special she was.

'What about other boyfriends? You know, at high school?'

'All-girls' boarding school.'

'Oh. Medical school?'

Clover had nodded slowly. 'Two guys—not at the same time, I might add.'

Brandon had smiled. 'Good to know. What ended it?'

'My father. He didn't approve.'

'So you broke up with them?'

She'd shaken her head. 'No. They broke up with me *after* my father had had a little...chat with them.'

'Ah. So when he approved of this other guy, you thought—why not?'

'Exactly. It was a mistake.'

'So what did he say when you broke it off with his man of choice?'

Clover had shrugged again. 'I don't know. We didn't discuss it.' With that, he'd seen the shutters come down on her past as she'd vigorously continued to sand their billy-cart.

Now as they chatted and laughed with their friends, other people pulling up chairs so they ended up being quite a large group, Brandon watched as Clover joined in the good-natured teasing, smiling brightly, her eyes alive with happiness.

In all their conversations he'd never heard her mention any close friends or any times when she'd gone down to the pub with her work colleagues for a quick drink at the end of a shift. She had confessed to being a workaholic and he wondered if that was because she was always searching for the next best way to garner some attention from her father.

Medical school, obstetric specialisation, working at a prestigious private hospital, dating a man her father approved of...what else had she done to try and gain some attention from the man who should be showering her with love?

The strong possessive spark he'd felt throughout the week only intensified as he began to piece together a rough picture of her life before they'd met. She was highly intelligent, resourceful, caring and extremely pretty but it was the way she laughed, the way she would gently caress his arm, the way she felt against his body, the way her mouth fitted perfectly with his own that was drawing him in. She *was* the whole package—

brains and beauty—and he knew he was close to being hooked.

When Saturday morning dawned bright and clear, Clover dressed in running shoes, long, sturdy denim jeans—as per Brandon's instructions—and was wearing a special red T-shirt that had 'Lewisville Billy-Cart Participant' printed on the front and a number on the back. It wasn't just any number...it was *her* number. She was just finishing a cup of coffee when Brandon came bounding in through the front door of his mother's house.

'You're up! Great. Ready for the best day of your life?'

'Ready,' she confirmed, and saluted. Brandon laughed and drew her close into his arms before giving her a good-morning kiss.

'I missed you,' he murmured near her ear.

'Likewise,' she responded, then kissed him again, before drawing back and pointing to the number on the back of her T-shirt. 'Look! I have a number.'

'Yep. I'm five and you're six.'

'I like six. *I'm* number six.' She giggled. 'I have

a number.' Clover clapped her hands with great delight. 'I've never had a number before.'

'What does that mean?' Brandon poured himself a quick cup of coffee, knowing his mother was already out and about in the town, helping to set things up and keep things moving. He sipped his drink, smiling at the way a simple T-shirt had made Clover so happy.

'I means I'm finally a part of something big and great and awesome. I'm "in the know". I'm one of the cool kids for a change.'

'Cool kids?'

She waved his words away and stacked her empty cup in the dishwasher. 'You know what I mean.'

'I think I do. You're excited at joining in the fun.'

'Oh, no. I'm not just *joining in*. I *joined in* at Ruby's wedding. No. Today isn't about *joining in*.'

'It's not?'

'No. Today *I* am a *participant*.' She clapped her hands again and Brandon simply couldn't help himself and drew her to him once more, infected by her happiness. 'I helped *build* that billy-cart, even though I can't quite believe it.'

'I'm glad we're doing this together.'

'So am I and I love that we're the red team and we wear matching T-shirts—'

'With numbers on the back,' he quickly interjected.

'Exactly! While we race down the street at goodness only knows how fast, trying to balance and hold on and not fracture half the bones in our bodies. And I'm so excited!'

'Unlike the first test run the other day when you were terrified to get on and then squealed all the way from start to finish?' he asked rhetorically.

'I have never done *anything* like this before.' She leaned up and kissed him, sighing against his warm, comforting and protective arms. 'Thank you, Brandon.'

'For...?'

'Asking me to be your partner. For including me. For getting me a T-shirt that makes me feel like I truly belong for the first time in my life. You're amazing.' She kissed him again and this time, before she could draw back, he slid a hand around and up the centre of her back, urging her to stay closer as he deepened the kiss.

Outside, Ned Finnegan, dressed in a red top, red shorts, flip-flops and also wearing a Santa beard and wide-brimmed hat, was trying to call everyone to order using a bull-horn, and as it squeaked, Clover and Brandon drew apart, both of them blocking their ears against the sound.

'Time to go,' Brandon said, and Clover nodded eagerly, heading for the door. 'Wait a moment. You forgot this.'

When Clover turned to see what he was holding up, she couldn't help but laugh. In his hands Brandon held two red Santa hats but they weren't of the usual nightcap variety. No, these were red Akubra hats with a sprig of wattle on the band and Christmas tinsel around the broad rims.

'Don't forget your Santa hat, number six.'

Clover allowed him to place it on her head. 'It's perfect. Did you decorate them especially for us?' She flicked her long braid down her back, getting her hair well out of the way.

'I did,' Brandon replied, and once more found

himself staring at her luscious lips. He took a step closer, his gaze never leaving her face as he angled his head down, twisting to angle it more so he didn't knock the hat from her head. Slowly, slowly, he continued in her direction, Clover licking her lips in delighted anticipation, then Ned gabbled something into the bull-horn, the only words Clover really able to process being 'To the starting line, please.'

Brandon pulled back and shoved his own hat onto his head. 'That's our cue.' Taking her hand in his, they left Viola's house and headed to the marshalling area, where a few of the younger kids were guarding their billy-cart.

Clover couldn't believe the number of people who had turned up for the race, everyone sporting something Christmassy, whether it was earrings, flashing brooches, reindeer ears or a Santa hat. Everyone was getting into the spirit of Christmas. The scent of sausages on a barbecue was starting to fill the air, with people swatting away flies with tassels of tinsel and drinking cool drinks. Stalls were set up along one side of the road.

'It really is a social calendar event,' she told him.

'Sure is. It's Christmas, plus it's also a fund-raising event. All the money raised today goes to support the village in Tarparnii where I worked for six months. PMA is looking to set up another medical clinic there but first the sanitation and supply of fresh water needs to be addressed so I'll be heading over for a two-week vacation once Ruby and Hamilton return in February to help build the well.'

'You're going to *build* the well?'

'Well, not by myself but with other people helping, sure.' He slung and arm around her shoulders. 'I'm not just a pretty face, you know.'

Clover smiled. 'I know that but you really do give and give, not just money but practical support. This is what it's all about. Being a part of something, of a community, of *really* helping.'

She sighed with delight. Finally, she'd found someone who understood what she'd been wanting to do all along, to use her skills and knowledge to really make a difference somewhere. 'It's a lovely idea.' She shook her head in bemusement. 'Everyone here really does care.'

'You sound surprised.'

'I guess I'm not used to people simply helping others without wanting anything in return.'

Brandon stared at her. 'You really have had a different upbringing.'

Clover stood her ground, holding his gaze but still feeling highly self-conscious when Brandon looked at her in such a way. She wanted him to see down into her soul, to see she was a good person, to see that she loved being in Lewisville. She wanted so desperately for him to accept her for who she was, rather than be like everyone else in her life who always saw her as the heiress to the Sampson fortune.

She knew her father and Xavier tolerated her desire to work as a doctor but they had always expected her to give up work after her marriage, to take her rightful place as patroness of many different organisations, holding fundraisers, attending lunches.

As Xavier had put it, 'Behaving like the heiress you are. One day your father will pass away and you'll inherit his shares in the Sampson Corporation. You need to be ready for that and you will be because I'll be right by your side, instructing you every step of the way.'

Clover didn't want that. She didn't want the label. She didn't want the fortune. She didn't want to give up her job. She didn't want to just throw money at people but instead help them in a hands-on way.

Brandon had done that when he'd gone to Tarparnii, working in a village that he and the rest of the Lewisville community had pledged to support. The people out here had their own problems and issues and often didn't have much money to spare but when they all pulled together, supporting and helping each other, a little bit could go a very long way and she admired that immensely.

As she continued to look into Brandon's gorgeous blue eyes, Ned gabbled something into his bull-horn that sounded as though the first race—the one for twelve-year-olds—was about to start.

'Let's go and watch,' she suggested, and he nodded, the two of them making their way to the sidelines to cheer on the competitors.

Clover saw Lacey Millar and her husband standing on the opposite side of the road and waved, the couple returning her greeting. Clover watched the smile on Lacey's face, noting it didn't quite meet her eyes.

'Something's happening,' she murmured, giving Lacey's abdomen a quick visual scan. Low and tight.

'Sorry? Did you say something?' Brandon asked, dipping his head so his ear was closer to her mouth.

'It's fine. Nothing.' She waved his words away and focused her attention on the race about to start, clapping and cheering along with everyone else.

There were a few cuts and scratches as people came off their billy-carts but on the whole there were no serious broken bones or anything like that and soon it was time for Clover and Brandon to take their places.

They changed their hats for proper racing helmets and donned protective knee-pads, elbow-pads, shin-pads, mouthguards and gloves. Safety first. It was almost eleven o'clock in the morning and the sun was now starting to beat down on them, warm and strong. It didn't matter because it was time for the real race, not just a practice one, and Clover could feel her nervous tension beginning to rise.

'Are you feeling OK?' Brandon asked, having to yell a little due to the helmets they were wearing. Clover made the 'OK' signal with her thumb and forefinger. 'Hey, I have a surprise for you,' he said, and urged her around to the rear of the cart, where he pulled off a sheet of green paper to reveal their names.

'Ta-dah!' He held out his hands, indicating the surprise he had for her. Clover stared in delighted amazement. There they were, their names—Clover and Brandon—intertwined with an ampersand in the middle, linking the names together. *Clover & Brandon*. She was deeply touched and lifted the visor of her helmet to gaze up into his eyes.

'Thank you. I *love* it.' I love you, she silently added, and breathed in the definitive knowledge to herself. She *loved* him. She *loved* Brandon. She could finally admit it to herself.

He smiled and nodded, wanting to remove the helmets and the rest of their protective gear and hold her close against his body, but it was time to start the race and so he winked at her before they took their places.

Clover's heart was beating wildly, not only from the lovely surprise he'd painted onto the back of their cart but because she'd just admitted to herself that she was in love with him. She hadn't wanted to think about her feelings too much but now she was forced to admit that she'd been in love with him for quite a while. What a time to discover she was in love!

She climbed into the billy-cart, her adrenaline beginning to pump as she shifted forward into position, ensuring she'd left enough room for Brandon to jump in after pushing them up to speed.

'Go get 'em, Clover and Brandon,' Viola cheered. Ned put the bull-horn to his mouth and began the countdown. It was still impossible to understand a word he was saying but as the actual starting signal was an air-horn, there was no chance they'd miss that. Brandon could only push for a certain distance, which was marked by a line further down the road, then he had to jump on behind Clover and see if they could make it to the finishing line first.

The green cart with red racing stripes was primed and ready to go and so when the air-horn sounded, Clover found herself letting out a squeal of excitement as Brandon began to push. She didn't look at the other racers, instead focus-ing herself on the task at hand.

After what seemed like an age, Brandon jumped in behind her, his strong arms coming around her to assist with the steering as they sped down the street. Clover tried to lower her head, as they'd practised so often, imagining for one brief moment that she was a luge athlete at the winter Olympics.

As she curved her back, Brandon's chest pressed into it, his arms tightening on the steer-ing rope, his legs alongside hers, so close and so confined and so intimately delightful. She didn't care whether they came first or last, being this close to the man of her heart made her feel like a winner.

Before she knew it, Brandon was angling the cart, both of them leaning to the side, but they must have leaned too far as in the next moment they tipped out of the cart, Clover landing on top of Brandon, their arms and legs sprawled and intertwined with each other's.

Brandon was shaking and Clover shifted, instantly concerned in case he'd hurt himself, but when she twisted around to look at his face she discovered he was laughing. A smile lit up her eyes and she grinned back at him, chuckling at what they'd just accomplished. She untangled her limbs from his and removed the helmet. 'That was completely awesome!'

'It was.' He sat up, removing his helmet and looking into her eyes. 'The most fun I've had in a long time. Ruby's always so competitive.'

Clover raised an eyebrow. 'And you're not?'

Brandon slowly shook his head. 'It doesn't matter if we come first or not, being with you, having fun with you, that's winning as far as I'm concerned.'

She smiled and touched a gloved hand tenderly to his cheek. 'That's one of the nicest thing anyone's ever said to me.'

Brandon leaned a little closer, his gaze centred

on her mouth for a split second before he met her eyes once more. 'Then remind me to say lots of nice things to you in future.' His words were soft as he continued to lean towards her.

Clover closed her eyes, waiting in anticipation for his lips to meet hers. She didn't care where she was or what was happening in her life, she wanted Brandon to kiss her now more than anything. They'd survived the billy-cart race and Brandon was talking about a future…a future for them together?

Clover didn't want to get her hopes up as she'd been let down far too many times before. She pushed the thought from her mind and focused on his mouth, silently willing him to hurry up because she wasn't sure she could wait any longer for one of his spectacular kisses.

'And the winners are…the red team!' Ned announced through the bull-horn, which miraculously seemed to be working now. At the mention of their team and the round of applause that accompanied the announcement, Brandon jerked back and Clover looked around to discover all eyes were on them.

He helped her to her feet and they accepted the congratulations of their friends and family. Viola ran towards them, her arms held wide. She embraced them both together.

'That was so exciting. One of the best runs ever made. So fast—and although Parker and Damien were fast, too, you just pipped them at the post, so to speak. I can't believe you won!' Viola was filled with excitement and continued to chatter on, telling them how pleased his father would have been that Brandon had finally won a race after all these years.

'And we can display the trophy at the clinic so everyone can see it, especially as it belongs to both of you,' Viola continued, as Clover and Brandon removed their protective gear and cleared their poor billy-cart off the road. 'Or do we keep it at the new maternity care centre? It's a dilem—'

'Clover! Clover!' A loud cry came from Damien Millar, who was beckoning them both over to where Lacey was sitting on the ground with the sun beating down on her, holding her belly and panting. Damien was quickly pulling

off all his protective gear and looking at his wife
as though he wasn't sure what to do. 'Clover!' he
shouted again, and Clover hurried to Lacey's side,
kneeling down and pressing a hand to the other
woman's abdomen.

'Is it happening?' Lacey asked as she gritted
her teeth in pain. 'Or is it just Braxton-Hicks'?'

'It's happening.' She turned to look at Brandon. 'Looks as though we have our first birth at
the maternity centre with or without equipment.
This little one's coming and he's not waiting for
anyone.'

'He's early,' Lacey stated. 'I can't go yet.'

'It looks as though Junior has other plans,' Clover countered.

CHAPTER TEN

GEOFFREY and Joan brought the ambulance stretcher over so they could transfer Lacey to the maternity centre. Quite a few people cheered them on as they moved through the crowd, wishing Lacey luck as they went. Clover was warmed by the caring community.

'Will it be OK, Clover?' Lacey asked, concern in her tone and worry etched on her brow. Damien was beside her, holding her hand. They entered the clinic and took Lacey through to a delivery room near the rear of the clinic.

'Everything will be fine,' Clover confirmed, her voice resonating pure calm and control.

'What do you need?' Geoffrey asked, after they'd transferred Lacey off the stretcher.

'I need Joan, Brandon, some cool air flowing through the centre and a bit of privacy,' she told him.

'Consider it done.' With that, Geoffrey wheeled the stretcher out of the room.

'*Very* well trained,' Clover couldn't help remark to Joan, the two women sharing a smile.

They all pulled on gowns to cover their clothing before Clover turned her focus to Lacey, who was lying back on the delivery bed, watching every move Clover made like a hawk.

'Now, Lacey. I need you to remember what we've talked about. We discussed what would happen if the baby came early and we know what to do. We're not going to panic.' Clover put her hand on Lacey's shoulder as the contraction eased. 'We're going to keep you comfortable and relaxed and let your body tell you what it wants to do.'

Clover's tone was soothing, caring and once again Brandon was struck by the way she could put people at ease, calm them down, which was exactly what Lacey needed right now.

'Remember, you're not in Broken Hill. Damien's here and Brandon, Joan and I will be caring for you both to the best of our abilities. This centre is all about providing for mother and babe, about making you feel as comfortable as possible.' While she spoke, concentrating on putting Lacey's mind at rest, Brandon and Joan rushed around like little worker ants, setting things up and getting ready.

'Now, it looks as though your waters have broken and—' As Clover started talking, Lacey began groaning again, her body tensing as the next contraction hit. 'That's it. Breathe through it. Squeeze the life out of Damien's hand if necessary. It's all right. He has another one.'

As the contraction began to subside, Clover took off Lacey's shoes and massaged her feet. 'There are pressure points here that help you to really let go of everything so just lie back and close your eyes. Conserving energy between contractions can really help.'

'Is there time for medication?' she asked.

'I'll do an exam in a minute once Joan's helped you into something a little more comfortable and practical for delivering a baby,' she answered.

Joan did exactly that, helping Lacey into a pale pink hospital gown. 'For now, though, we're going to use the new baby heart monitor and just see what sort of heartbeat the little fella is kicking out.'

Clover turned to look for the piece of equipment she needed and found Brandon holding it out for her. 'Thank you,' she said with a quick smile, then turned back to her patient.

Brandon couldn't get over how calm and in control she was. This was her speciality. She'd already delivered hundreds of babies over the years, whereas, he had to confess, assisting with a delivery was not one of his favourite things to do as so much could go wrong, especially out here in the Outback.

But now, thanks to Clover's brilliant idea, they had this little maternity centre where Lacey could have her baby closer to home with her husband by her side. She could stay on here for a few weeks, if she wanted and learn how to bath her baby, how to feed him, how to change his nappy and settle him down to sleep at night. She would be supported by the older women in the community and Brandon knew his mother would be one of the first volunteers for the job.

Getting both mothers and babies into a routine

before they went home would definitely set the young families of this community off to a good start.

'So how are you feeling?' Clover asked after she'd completed her exam.

'Like another contraction is coming,' Lacey replied, every muscle in her body tensing as the pain hit. Clover guided Lacey with her breathing then, and once the contraction started to subside, Clover did another exam.

'You're fully dilated. Have you been having any sort of contractions over the past few days?'

'Yes,' Lacey admitted. 'I'd read up about Braxton-Hicks' contractions and thought it was just that.'

'Yes, they were, but those contractions let you know that things are starting to move.'

'I was going to call you and ask you if that's what was going on but I just didn't want him to come out now. He's four weeks early.'

'He's going to be fine…and fast by the look of things. Your contractions are just over two minutes apart. Chances are you've been in the early stages of labour since yesterday.'

'That's fast!'

'It is for a first baby but not to worry.'

'So…this is really it? I'm…in… labour?' Lacey was stunned.

Clover's smile was bright. 'You're in labour,' she confirmed. It wasn't the first time she'd had a conversation like this with a woman about to deliver. Nine times out of ten they'd turn up at the hospital concerned they might be in labour, but even after they'd started pushing, they'd found it difficult to accept that after nine or so months the labour was *actually happening*.

Clover held the foetal heart monitor to Lacey's abdomen and listened closely, her gaze meeting Brandon's as together they mentally counted the beats. Brandon nodded, as though silently confirming what Clover was thinking.

'What is it?' Damien asked, having witnessed the exchange between the two doctors.

'The beats aren't as fast as we'd like,' Clover said. Her tone was still calm and controlled but Brandon could tell she was mentally running through what she'd need in case of an emergency C-section. They may be in the new maternity centre, they may be delivering their first baby on the premises, but the humidi-cribs weren't due to arrive until after Christmas and as this little one was early, it meant they all needed to improvise.

'What…what does that mean?' Lacey asked.

'It means the baby could go into distress if we don't deliver him or her sooner rather than later,' Clover returned, as she checked Lacey's vitals, pleased everything was within normal parameters. Once that was done, she listened to the baby's heart rate again.

'It's a little lower than before.'

Lacey looked at her husband and squeezed his hand again. 'Something's wrong, Damien. Something's wrong with our baby.'

'It's all right, Lacey.' Clover could hear the panic beginning to rise in Lacey's tone. 'We can deal with this togeth—' But before she could finish her sentence Lacey let out a loud cry and started to push. 'Right. That's the first push so that's our cue.' She did another exam and could see the head was starting to crown.

'Joan, Brandon, I need you to prepare a make-shift humidi-crib and oxygen box.'

'Oxygen box?' Lacey asked, fear creeping into her tone.

'Precaution. I like to be set up for any eventuality. We have most things but for those we don't, we'll simply organise an alternative. Remember, Brandon's been working overseas in Tarparnii where, from what I've read in articles, women can sometimes have their babies on the side of the road. He knows how to improvise.'

Brandon was pleased to hear she had so much confidence in him, especially as obstetrics was her speciality. He could also tell she was trying not to startle Lacey too much but also wanted the new mother to know that, as professionals, they had everything under control. He left the room, intent on doing what Clover required.

'What we need you to do, Lacey,' Clover continued, 'is to concentrate on bringing this gorgeous little one into the world. I need you to keep breathing and listening to what I say. I might need you to push really hard or I might need you *not* to push—which is the most difficult thing to do in the world, especially when all your muscles are contracting and urging you to push. Just listen to my instructions and we'll take care of the rest.'

After the next contraction, when Lacey once more couldn't help but push, poor Damien's hand being squeezed so hard it was turning purple, Clover once more checked the baby's heart rate, disappointed to find it still decreasing. That wasn't good. She checked Lacey's blood pressure and found that it was well within normal limits. Something was affecting the baby, something bad, and Clover went over different scenarios in her mind.

'Good, Lacey. You're doing a fantastic job.'

'And the baby's heart rate?' Lacey asked. 'Why is it so slow? What do you think it is?'

Clover knew at a time like this that plain speaking was the best tack to take. 'Well, the most common cause of a decreased heart rate is that the cord is wrapped around the baby's neck. When the contractions start, that cord can become rather tight, but we'll sort it out. Just keep listening to my directions, OK? That's the most important thing at the moment.'

Lacey met Clover's eyes and nodded. 'I will,' she promised.

After several more contractions, with Lacey dutifully focusing on her breathing, Damien mopping the perspiration from her brow and offering her sips of water, Clover announced the baby's head was almost out.

'A few more nice big pushes. Come on, let's breathe together.' Clover counted down, breathing in time with Lacey.

She heard Brandon re-enter the room and glanced across at him for a split second, pleased when she received a thumbs-up and a big encouraging grin from him. It was exactly what she'd needed right at that point in time. She was concerned for the baby, well aware they were missing a lot of equipment but not wanting to alarm the mother too much.

Lacey gritted her teeth and pushed, yelling her frustration and pain into the room. 'Good. Well done,' Clover encouraged. 'One more big push and the head will be out. Then I'll be able to check the baby's neck. One more big one. Come on, Lacey. You can do it. Snatch a breath and *push*!'

Lacey followed Clover's instructions. 'Excellent. The head is out. Well done. Now comes the hard part. I need you not to push. Even if you feel like it. You must resist the urge to push. Damien? Help Lacey with her breathing.'

'On it,' Damien replied, completely focused on his wife.

'How are you doing, Brandon?' Clover asked, as she carefully felt the baby's neck for the cord. There it was. Wrapped firmly about the little one's neck. With deft fingers Clover managed to ease the cord over the baby's head.

'I want to push. *I want to push*,' Lacey demanded.

'Don't push,' Clover said firmly.

'Breathe. Breathe.' Joan came alongside Lacey and took her other hand. 'Breathe and squeeze all your pain into our hands,' she encouraged, with poor Damien groaning in agony as his wife once more squeezed his hand. 'That's it. Nice shallow breaths,' Joan encouraged.

'Almost there. Just a moment longer.' The cord

was wrapped twice around the baby's neck and Clover gritted her teeth as she unlooped it the second time around, checking and double-checking that everything was now fine as the baby's shoulders started to rotate.

'Done. The cord is off.' There was a collective exhalation of breath at this news. 'Push when you're ready, Lacey.' But no sooner had Clover said the words than Lacey was pushing as though her life depended on it. The baby's shoulders appeared and a short while later the baby boy slid into Clover's waiting arms.

'It's a boy! It's a *boy*!' Damien whooped, and laughed. 'We have a son!'

'Is he all right?' Lacey asked, trying to raise her head. 'Is he breathing? How's his heart rate?'

'Just a moment,' Clover said as she and Brandon worked quickly to clamp the cord. 'Sorry, Damien. No time for you to do the honours,' she went on, as Brandon cut the cord and then took the baby, rubbing the little blue-tinged body to stimulate blood flow as well as remove the vermix.

'He's not breathing,' Brandon stated as Clover

drew up an injection of Vitamin K to administer to Lacey to avoid post-partum haemorrhaging before the third stage of labour began.

'Clear the mouth and nose.'

She had hoped for the care centre to be completely set up before the first birth but with no humidi-crib, suction machine or oxygen boxes, they had to do their best. It was great to see she could rely on Brandon, that when it came to crunch time he was right in there, adapting and changing things around so they had exactly what they needed.

Somehow he'd managed to find a metal frame that looked as though it had come from the inside of a filing cabinet. Next, he'd wrapped the metal frame in plastic sandwich wrap to make a clear area for them to pump oxygen into so the baby could get what it needed. What a clever man.

'Doing it,' Brandon returned, as he carefully wiped the baby's mouth and nose out with a swab and a cotton bud.

Being an Outback GP often meant doing things either the old-fashioned way or adapting to the surroundings in order to get the job done. The baby still wasn't breathing and although he could do mouth-to-mouth resuscitation, he decided to try one more thing first, the old-fashioned way of getting a baby to breathe, the way that had been good enough for him and countless other babies throughout centuries. He lifted the little boy up by the feet, tipped him upside down and smacked his bottom.

There was a moment of complete and utter silence as everyone seemed to hold their breath, then…the most glorious sound, one of a soft, indignant cry, filled the air as Lacey's and Damien's little boy registered his protest.

Breathing a collective sigh of relief and happiness, everyone smiled. Brandon continued to care for the baby, ensuring the oxygen saturations were at the correct level as he placed him into the improvised oxygen tent, keeping him as warm as possible.

He looked over his shoulder at Clover, who was still attending to the weeping Lacey. Their gazes met and held, and together they shared a smile of relief, of success, of mutual admiration. After checking his little boy out, Damien had headed outside and used Ned's bull-horn to announce the news to the rest of the town.

'I have a son!'

Everyone in the delivery room smiled warmly at the loud cheer that went up from outside and later, with Lacey under Joan's watchful eye and as little baby Orsonn was improving by leaps and bounds, enjoying his first feed and cuddle with his parents, Clover removed her gown and stepped out onto the back veranda of the centre for a moment of peace.

'Mind if I join you?' Brandon's deep tones washed over her and she turned, a smile already on her lips, and held out her hand to him. 'First baby born in the new maternity care centre. Orsonn Millar has himself a place in the Lewisville history books.'

He went to her, sliding his arms around her waist and holding her close, both of them content to just hold each other. Clover couldn't believe how incredible, how right, how perfect it felt to be exactly where she was.

Lifting her head, her heart hammering wildly

against her ribs, she looked into his gorgeous blue eyes, eyes she would never tire of. 'Brandon?'

He frowned a little. 'Something wrong? You look really worried.'

'Not worried. A bit apprehensive but that can't be helped.'

'What is it? What's wrong?'

'Nothing's wrong,' she replied, her smile widening as she gently shook her head. 'Everything's right. Everything is *so* right, *so* perfect. I had no idea life could be like this.'

'I know.' After Lynn's betrayal, he'd wondered if he'd ever be able to trust again and yet, standing here, holding Clover in his arms, he felt wonderful. 'Come on,' he said after a moment. 'Let's go get a nice cool drink. I think we deserve it.'

Her smile was bright as she nodded, and after checking on the newest addition to the Lewisville community, ensuring that mother and babe were fine and with Joan shooing them both away saying she'd keep an eye on things while they went and had a celebratory iced slushy, they left the maternity care centre and stepped out into the heat.

'Here you go,' Brandon said, as he placed Clover's red tinselled hat on her head. 'Don't want you getting burnt.' As they walked towards the cool-drink stand, they were both stopped along the way by several people, being congratulated and thanked for a job well done. Some people shook her hand, others—namely Viola—embraced Clover in an enormous hug.

'We're so lucky to have you here, Clover. Our first baby, born in the new care centre. It's all just perfect.'

After a while Clover lost sight of Brandon as she was still being asked all sorts of details by all sorts of people wanting to know how heavy little Orsonn was or how big his head was or how long he was. She presumed Brandon had made it to the drink stand but after she'd finished answering several questions and recounting the way Lacey had been amazing during the birth, Clover headed to the stall but found he wasn't there.

She searched the crowd for him, smiling and nodding to other people as they walked past, but still there was no sign of him. Perhaps he'd gone to the pub but after she'd checked, still unable to find him, she'd bumped into Geoffrey.

'Have you seen Brandon?'

'Yes. He's out the back of the pub, talking to some guy who's just passing by for the day.'

'Thanks.' Clover headed around the side of the pub down towards the small outdoor beer garden which was rarely used as most people preferred the air-conditioning inside the pub. As she rounded the corner, going up the two steps that led to the veranda covered deck, she heard Brandon's voice.

'Is that right? Wow. That's…a lot. I had no idea.' He had his back to her and she smiled, knowing it was just like him to make people passing through his town feel welcome—just as he'd done with her when they'd first met. He was such an incredible man, caring, giving, thoughtful. She couldn't see the man he was talking to as Brandon's gorgeously large shoulders were blocking her view.

'So this is where you're hiding,' she remarked, coming to stand beside him. It was only then she glanced across at the other man, ready to say hello, to be polite and shake hands and do her bit of welcoming a stranger to the amazing town of Lewisville—when she realised she already knew the stranger in question. 'Xavier!' Her jaw dropped open as she felt the blood drain from her body. 'Wh-what are you doing here?'

CHAPTER ELEVEN

SHE looked from Brandon to Xavier and back again, her mouth going dry as her heart hammered out a mortified rhythm.

'Clover. There you are.'

'Xavier, here, was just telling me all about your father's corporation. The *Sampson* Corporation, and how you're the sole heiress to the entire thing.'

Xavier nodded, clearly not realising what he'd just done. 'That's right. Our Clover is one special woman.'

'Oh, yes. *Our* Clover is certainly…*special.*'

Clover could hear the veiled pain hidden beneath Brandon's words. She met his gaze, unable to hide the truth. 'Brandon, I—'

'And all the time she's been in town, helping us out, joining in with all sorts of community events, we've all been none the wiser that we had a millionaire in our midst.'

Xavier chuckled. 'She does enjoy her little projects, helping others out with her doctoring skills. I have no idea why. There's no reason in the world why she should work but she does insist on it.'

'Maybe she likes playing games. Is that right, *Clover*? Do you enjoy tricking others?'

Clover sighed and shook her head sadly, seeing the pain and anger in Brandon's eyes. He had every right to be angry and she knew now she should have made more of an effort to tell him the truth before something like this happened. She looked from Brandon to Xavier. 'How did you find me?'

Xavier tut-tutted. 'Darling, I'm a man of means and intelligence. I think I can track down my fiancée when she decides to wander off.'

'Fiancée?' Brandon kept his cool, his tone dry and filled with pain. 'Well, well, well. It's just one surprise after another. That's something else *our* Clover failed to mention.' He pierced Clover with a harsh look before turning his attention back to the city dweller, dressed in suit trousers, a crisp white shirt and university tie. 'Tell me, Xavier, how long have the two of you been engaged?'

'Let's see, I proposed in early July when we were in Port Douglas. The wedding's at the end of February and after her father's Christmas Eve party—which is spectacular, by the way—we'll be heading into major planning mode.' Xavier looked at Clover. 'My PAs have already arranged your dress fittings with the designer and drawn up the preliminary guest list. It's going to be the event of the year!'

Clover stared at Xavier as though he was completely insane. 'Wh—?' She stopped and shook her head, her hands clenched into fists by her sides. 'How da—?' She stopped again and gritted her teeth.

'Don't grind your teeth, Clover. I don't want a bride with a crooked smile.' Xavier laughed and nodded at Brandon. 'Am I right? I'm right, aren't I?'

'Ugh!' Clover had had enough and she was simply far too furious with Xavier to even begin to form coherent sentences. Throwing her arms in the air, she spun on her heel and stormed off, furious with Xavier and fearful of what Brandon was making of all of this. Tears stung at her eyes as she took the short cut around the rear of the buildings, hoping to make it back to Viola's place, where she could hibernate in her room until she calmed down.

'Clover?' She heard Brandon call her name just as she reached Viola's back door and she turned to face him. 'When were you going to tell me you were engaged? Or weren't you going to bother with that little detail?'

A fresh surge of anger exploded over her as she stared at him, then she shook her head and went inside.

'Avoiding the truth again?' Brandon followed her into the house, stopping in the laundry as she stood there, glaring at him, hands on her hips.

'I'm not avoiding the truth. I never have.'

'Yet you never thought to mention that you were engaged? Or is that just one of those minor details you've been concealing from me?' He shook his head. 'I knew it. I knew you were hiding things from me. I kept telling myself that you couldn't possibly be as perfect and glorious as you appeared to be. So calm and controlled all the time with that mesmerising hint of aloofness. I knew I was a fool to trust you and yet I let my guard down and once again fell for a woman who can't help but lie to me.'

'I have never lied to you,' Clover returned. Ordinarily, she avoided confrontation wherever possible but since coming to Lewisville she'd discovered a new Clover. Here she'd been valued, accepted and, as such, her personal confidence had grown. She didn't want Brandon to think she'd been lying to him when she hadn't.

'I applied for the job under my professional name—Clover Farraday. Farraday was my mother's maiden name. My full name, if you care to know it, is Clover Beatrice Gertrude Hazel Farraday-Sampson, not that it should make any difference. And as far as not mentioning I was engaged, well, that's easy because I'm *not* engaged. I never *have* been engaged to Xavier. The ridiculous man simply refuses to take no for an answer.'

Clover turned and stormed down the corridor

towards her room. Brandon followed, standing in the doorway.

'So you're saying that man didn't even propose?'

'What's that got to do with anything? Why can't you believe me?'

'And I suppose you're not the daughter of a multi-billionaire who has so much money he could buy the entire country if he wanted to?'

'It's not my fault who my father is and as I've already told you, we don't exactly get along.' She shook her head and planted her hands on her hips.

'So are you really worth millions? Was coming here to Lewisville just your way of filling in time before your big society wedding?'

'I don't believe this.' She covered her face with her hands, knocking off her tinsel-covered hat.

'Neither do I because you're still avoiding the question,' he growled. 'Why didn't you tell me about your father? About who he is?'

'Because in the past, every time I've been interested in a man, my father has interfered by buying them off.'

'What? You mean he paid them money to *stop* dating you?'

'That's exactly what I mean. Everyone has their price, Brandon.' She spread her arms wide. 'Do you have any idea how it feels to have a person you thought you cared about, that you thought you could one day really come to love, take a better offer and ditch you—ditch you because of money?'

'Yes, as a matter of fact, I do know what it feels like. Lynn may not have ditched me for a fortune but she certainly ditched me because I wasn't good enough.'

'Then you know how worthless your life feels, how betraying, how belittling it is.'

'Yes.'

'And that's why I didn't tell you who my father was. That's why I don't tell anyone. That's why I changed my name.'

Brandon blinked once. 'You thought he'd buy me off?'

'Everyone has their price,' she reiterated, and she hadn't been able to bear the thought that he would leave her—just like the other men she'd cared about.

'Even after we came to mean something to each other, you still didn't trust me,' Brandon stated, and shook his head. Clover thought she might break down and sob right then and there at the look of disgust in his eyes. 'You know, every time I asked you about your life in Sydney, you'd give me a short answer and change the subject.'

She dropped her hands and shook her head. 'I don't like talking about my life for that exact reason and as I *have* told you, it was hardly a happy life.' She was getting hot under the collar now and raised her voice—something she'd never done before, especially during an argument.

'A life you still can't bring yourself to talk about.'

'It's my past. I can't change it.' She clenched her jaw so tightly her head really began to pound. 'Why is it so important?'

'Because it is,' Brandon yelled in exasperation.

Clover blinked once, twice, unable to believe he was yelling at her. She looked away, desperate to hold back the tears that were threatening to erupt. She clenched her hands and tried to swallow, needing to maintain control over her emotions. The last thing she wanted to do right now was to cry, to have Brandon think she was using tears, her feminine wiles, to get around him. He either could accept her for who she was or he couldn't. It really was that simple.

She pursed her lips and looked down at the floor then looked into his eyes. 'I love you, Brandon, and that *is* the truth.' She bit her lip as she waited for his response to her declaration but he just stood there, glaring at her. Finally, he shook his head.

'I don't know how I can trust anything you say. You want to know what my "price" is? My price is freedom—from you.' With that, he turned and walked from her room. A second later, the front screen door banged shut—just as he'd shut her out of his life.

As the band started to play and the guests began to arrive, Clover pasted on a smile. Not for her father and certainly not for Xavier. This Christmas Eve party was a great fundraiser for welfare agencies where the rich came to this party, giving lots of money without having to rub shoulders with the poor. Yet the last thing she felt like doing was smiling—for she really had nothing to smile about.

Since Brandon had stomped out of his mother's house three days ago, Clover had changed her clothes, packed her bags and allowed Xavier to take her back to Sydney. She'd barely spoken a word to him during the entire chopper ride to Sydney, not that it had bothered Xavier, who had taken the opportunity to organise some more business. It was only when she'd finally been taken to her apartment that she'd allowed her emotions to have free rein.

Brandon hadn't believed in her. Brandon hadn't been able to accept her for who she was and it was that pain, that hurt, that had had her sobbing into her pillow for the past few nights.

On her first morning back in Sydney she'd sat on her balcony and watched the sunrise, annoyed with herself for failing to be moved by the beautiful sight, which had always managed to calm her down. It was then she realised that nothing mattered much any more simply because Brandon didn't love her.

Everything in life was just going through the motions and that was what she was doing tonight. Walking through her life as though it was a part in a play. She'd managed to arrange for one of her trusted OB/GYN colleagues to head to Lewisville over the Christmas period to fill in for her. After that, she'd sort out a more permanent replacement. There was no way Clover was leaving that town without obstetric support but neither was there any way she could go back and work alongside Brandon every day, knowing her heart would always be his when he didn't care for her. It would be too torturous.

She looked across the yard to where her father stood at the entrance to a large marquee, shaking hands with someone and having his photograph taken by a reporter. Since she'd arrived back in Sydney, they hadn't spoken. For some reason, that didn't bother her as much as it had in the past. Was it because she'd managed to find happiness in Lewisville? With Brandon? Even though it had been only for a short while, for one brief moment there, with her red number-six T-shirt on, she'd belonged.

'My PAs informed me this afternoon,' Xavier remarked as he came to stand beside her, 'that your engagement ring is finally perfect. I had to send it back twice because the diamond wasn't big enough. I'm having it sent over tonight as an early Christmas present for you. I think your father's scheduled a photo session for seven-thirty tomorrow morning.'

'Tomorrow's Christmas,' Clover pointed out, unable to believe Xavier was still persisting with this engagement.

'I know.'

'Xavier, what do you get if you marry me? I mean, what's your price?'

'My price! Honestly, Clover. Some days, you're incredibly vulgar.'

'Well...what is it? It has to be something. Everyone has a price.'

'Not me. I have plenty of money. That's one of the reasons your father gave his blessing to our engagement. The fact that he knows for sure I'm not a gold-digger.'

'But you are a snob and I'm going to say that your price is…prestige. You want prestige in being married into one of the wealthiest families in Australia. You want the Sampson name forever connected with your own.' She looked at his face and nodded. 'I'm right, too. I can see it in your eyes. That's the one thing my father's always been right about. Everyone has their price.' She turned to leave but stopped and levelled him with a direct look.

'And for the last time, we are *not* engaged, Xavier. I don't know how many times I have to say it but it may help you to know that I'm actually in love with another man and if I can ever get him to speak to me again, to give me the time of day once more, I will do whatever it takes to find a way to spend my life with him.'

As she turned and walked away, Clover realised that even *she* had a price.

Brandon stood in the lavishly lit gardens of the Sampson mansion, wondering how on earth he was supposed to find Clover in a throng of over a thousand people? He wasn't wearing a tuxedo, like every other man here, and with the way the women were dressed, in their latest designer clothes, dripping with jewels, he knew he stood out from the crowd.

The past three days—the three days since Clover had left Lewisville—had been the worst. Even when Lynn had left, he hadn't felt *this* bad. He snagged a drink from the tray of a passing waiter but even as he brought the glass to his lips, he decided he didn't want it after all. Nothing could quench his thirst any more. Nothing could fill his stomach. Nothing could help him sleep. Nothing could make him happy—and it was all because he'd been stupid enough to let Clover go.

Now it was Christmas Eve and over the past few days in Lewisville everything had been sparkly and bright and festive...and Clover had missed it. Far too often, he'd turned around to tell her something, to share a laugh, to hug her close, to kiss her...but she hadn't been there.

His life had been a shambles, cold, empty... pointless, which was why he'd strode from his bed earlier that morning, left a note for his mother and called in quite a few favours in order to get him to Sydney by tonight. It hadn't been easy but Clover was definitely worth it.

And now here he was, at her family mansion, and all he wanted was to find her. He didn't care about her father or the money or whether or not she was engaged to Xavier. She belonged with him. She belonged with him *in* Lewisville and he refused to leave Sydney until he'd told her that. He had a price, she'd been right about that, but it wasn't the price she'd thought.

Where on earth could she be?

As he walked purposefully through the garden towards the large marquee that had been set up with a dance floor and an orchestra, he couldn't help comparing this type of fundraising event to the ones they held in Lewisville. So incredibly different.

Did Clover like all this stuff? The fancy twinkle lights, the trees in the garden that had been decorated with large baubles and tinsel, and the orchestral version of classic Christmas carols? Glasses of champagne clinked near him and bow-tied waiters carried silver trays of food through the throng of people.

It certainly was a different world here and he could well imagine lonely little Clover attending many of these parties as a child, wearing a pretty dress and looking perfect but never allowed to move from a chair lest she mess up her dress or ruin her hair. His heart bled for all those warm and wonderful times she'd missed with her mother. His family may not have been excessively wealthy, but they'd been rich with the blessings of familial love.

Brandon continued to scan the crowd, not finding her anywhere. Perhaps he should have called ahead, letting her know he was coming. He'd been too focused on actually getting to Sydney, calling in a favour from his friend who flew the emergency helicopter and then paying double for the taxi to get him here as fast as possible.

At the door to the mansion he'd been denied entry as his name hadn't been on the guest list so he'd made a generous donation to tonight's charity and had reluctantly been permitted entry... and now he couldn't find her.

Raking a hand through his hair, he shook his head and decided to find a nice quiet corner where he could think through his next move. One thing was for sure, he wasn't leaving Sydney without talking to her.

As he made his way through the crowd, he spotted a small path leading down to a gazebo that overlooked a duck pond. With the hustle and bustle starting to ebb, he breathed a sigh of relief as he entered the gazebo.

'Brandon?'

He turned. 'Clover?'

And there she was. Sitting on a seat looking out at the duck pond.

'What are you doing here?'

'I've been looking for you.'

They spoke in unison as she stood and he took a step closer. His gaze travelled over her and even though there wasn't as much lighting here as there was behind them, he could well appreciate the exquisite red satin dress she wore, tied on one shoulder and leaving the other one bare. There was no need for a necklace as the bodice was adorned with sparkles of some sort. Her hair was secured in an elegant style that made her look regal and glorious.

Brandon was riveted to the spot, unable to take his eyes off her, and was fairly sure his jaw had hit the ground as he gaped at the stunning woman who had captured his heart.

'You look…amazing.'

'So do you.' With his jeans, running shoes and T-shirt that still fitted him to absolute perfection, he looked as gloriously handsome as he had the day they'd first met.

He laughed and shook his head as he pulled at his T-shirt. 'What? This ol' thing?'

Clover smiled and took a small step towards him. 'What are you doing here?' she asked again.

'I've come to grovel.'

'OK.'

He blinked once, surprised she was going to let him actually go through with it. Clover dug her nails into the palms of her hands, trying to stop the itching need to throw herself into his arms. She still couldn't believe he was actually there but now that he was, she wanted to hear what he had to say.

'I was an idiot.'

'Yes.'

'You really aren't going to make this easy, are you,' he stated.

'No.'

'Why?'

'Because you hurt me.'

'I know and I'm so sorry.' He raked a hand through his hair. 'I was just surprised to hear you were engaged—'

'*Not* engaged,' she said, pointing to herself.

'And I was hurt that you hadn't trusted me enough to tell me who your father really was.'

'It's not easy for me to open up because for far too long I've been ignored, shut out. My father, Xavier—they're the same. Neither of them listen to me. Neither of them ask me what it is *I* want to do with my life. That was different with you. You listened when I talked. You made me laugh, you made me feel as though I was a person of worth, not just a possession. You really do know me better than anyone else, Brandon. You know the *real* Clover because you didn't pressure me.'

'And yet when it came to crunch time, I *didn't* listen. That's why you left.'

'I've been ignored for most of my life.' Tears

began to glisten in her eyes. 'I couldn't bear to stay in Lewisville and be ignored by *you.*'

'Oh, Clover.' With that, he covered the distance between them and gathered her into his arms. She buried her head into his shoulder and held him close, never wanting to let him go again. 'I can't ignore you because if I do, I'd be ignoring my own heart.' He eased back from her. 'You have it, you know. You've had my heart since my sister's wedding when I couldn't help but kiss you.'

'That was one of the happiest nights of my life.'

He smiled down into her upturned face, dabbing at the corner of her eyes with his thumbs, tenderly brushing away the few tears that had spilled over. 'Mine, too.' He caressed her cheek. 'I love you, Clover Beatrice Hazel Gertrude Farraday-Sampson. I love every single part of you and I always will.'

Clover bit her lip, unable to believe this was really happening, that Brandon was really here, holding her in his arms, telling her he loved her.

'Marry me?' He swallowed and she was astonished to see nervousness reflected in his eyes.

Surely he knew how much she loved him? Surely he knew her answer would be yes to that heart-felt important question?

'Clover?' a male voice said from behind them, and both she and Brandon turned to find her father standing at the edge of the gazebo, looking at both of them. Brandon tightened his arms around Clover, indicating he wasn't about to let her go.

'What's going on?' Oswald asked as he looked from her to Brandon.

'Dad. I'd like you to meet my fiancé. My *real* fiancé,' she remarked, looking lovingly up at Brandon.

Brandon quickly held out one hand, the other still firmly around Clover's waist. Now that he'd found her, he wasn't letting her go. Oswald simply glanced at Brandon's hand as though it was covered with disease, before turning his attention once more to his daughter.

'You've done it again. Gone and got yourself mixed up with a hooligan. All right,' he sighed, and looked at Brandon. 'Name your price.'

Brandon shook his head and slid his ignored

hand back around Clover's waist. 'I don't have one, sir. Not one money can buy.'

'That's what they all say, boy.'

'It's true,' Clover remarked. 'Brandon can't be bought.'

'If it isn't money, what is it you want?' Oswald asked, ignoring his daughter.

'Well, sir. I've given it a lot of thought.'

'I bet you have. What is it? New house? New car?'

'No sir. My price...' Brandon looked down into Clover's gorgeous face '...is to spend the rest of my days making your daughter as happy as possible.'

Oswald frowned for a moment. 'Seriously. Get to the point. I have a speech to make soon.'

'I am serious.' Brandon tucked a loose tendril of hair behind Clover's ear. 'I love her with all my heart and I'm going to marry her.' He bent his head and brushed a kiss over her lips before looking at her father once more. 'I'm sorry if that disappoints you and of course both of us would like you to come to the wedding, but if you feel you're incapable of doing that one small thing for your only daughter, then we respect your decision.' He returned his attention to his gorgeous fiancée.

'Clover doesn't need to vie for your attention any more, Mr Sampson, because I willingly give her mine.' He brushed the backs of his fingers across her cheek. 'I do love you so, my Clover. I really do need you to be with me for ever.'

'Oh, Brandon.' She stood on tiptoe and kissed him warmly, forgetting her father, forgetting the party, forgetting everything except the way he made her feel.

'This is ridiculous.' Oswald was about to say more but was cut short when an aide came to tell him it was time for the speeches. 'We'll discuss this later,' he warned his daughter.

'No, Dad. We won't.' She looked at him, releasing Brandon just for a moment before crossing to her father's side and pressing a small, sad kiss on his cheek. 'I don't *need* you in my life any more, Dad. I *want* you in it, of course, but my price— the price I'd pay to get what I want—is to leave Sydney, leave my job, leave my entire past here and go to Lewisville with Brandon, where I *know* I truly belong.'

Oswald stared at his daughter, seeing her perhaps for the first time, but he didn't say anything. Instead, he walked away, leaving Brandon and Clover to their peace and solitude, something both of them were more than happy about.

'Are you all right?' Brandon asked, once more drawing her into the circle of his arms.

'Yes. It was time.'

'So...I take it you're definitely going to marry me?'

Clover smiled. 'What gave you that idea?'

'Perhaps it was the way you introduced me as your fiancé. Or maybe it was the way you kissed me...' He brushed a tantalising kiss across her lips and Clover couldn't help but smile. 'Or maybe it was the way you—' He didn't get to finish his sentence as she effectively silenced him with a kiss.

'You talk too much,' she murmured against his mouth.

'Then allow me to rectify the situation,' he returned, then Brandon lowered his head and captured her mouth in the most wonderful of kisses, filled with the promises of an incredible life together.

Finally, he raised his head and looked down into her beautiful face, both of them slightly breathless but incredibly happy. 'Merry Christmas, my love.'

'Yes, it is going to be a *very* merry Christmas!'

EPILOGUE

'THE wedding was held in the middle of the main street of the sleepy Outback town of Lewisville, cordoned off especially for the festivities. The bride, as is traditional, wore white, but not a designer gown as you would expect for the heiress to the Sampson Corporation. Instead, the simple yet elegant dress was hand-stitched by the groom's mother, Mrs Viola Goldmark. Mrs Goldmark will be using this opportunity to launch her new career as a seamstress later this year.'

Viola laughed, as did Ruby, playfully hitting her husband's arm to get him to stop. 'Oh, Hamilton.'

'What are you laughing at?' Clover asked as she and Brandon came to sit down at their table. Clover kicked off her shoes and allowed Brandon to pull her onto his lap.

'Hamilton and his brothers keep writing tomorrow's newspaper headlines, describing the society wedding that never was.'

'We're positive there are journalists lurking around the outskirts of town, peering at us all through binoculars and telephoto lenses,' Bartholomew Goldmark added. The entire clan had returned to Lewisville for another wedding, all of them delighting at seeing Brandon so happily settled with Clover.

Naturally, Clover had been only too delighted to resume her position as OB/GYN to Lewisville and surrounding districts. The maternity care centre was now fully operational, with all the equipment having arrived the week after Christmas. Clover had now delivered three babies in the centre and Viola and Marissa Mandocicelli were running daily programmes for young mothers, helping them to cope.

'I wish there had been something like this when I'd had my children,' Marissa had told her. 'You're a genius, Clover.'

'Yes, she is,' Brandon had agreed.

When the band began to play again, Brandon urged Clover up off his knee before scooping her up into his arms and carrying her towards the makeshift dance floor. 'Care to dance, Mrs Goldmark?' he asked as she slid provocatively down his body.

'I thought you'd never ask, Mr Goldmark.' And barefoot and in his arms, Clover was more than happy, more than satisfied, more than content to dance with the man of her dreams. Amazingly enough, her father had actually relented and attended her wedding, walking her down the bitumen road of Main Street towards the man who would forever be her husband.

'It's not too late to change your mind,' her father had murmured out of the corner of his mouth.

'Be quiet, Dad, and just keep smiling,' had been her reply.

'Do you know your father offered me another bribe five minutes before the ceremony?' Brandon remarked, and Clover eased back to look at him, raising an eyebrow. 'He tripled his original offer and, of course, I refused.'

She smiled. 'I gathered that, otherwise we wouldn't be standing here, dancing slowly and sensually together.'

'True…but it's what happened *after* I refused his final offer.'

'And what's that?'

'He shook my hand. The great and powerful Oz shook my hand.' Brandon held up the hand in question and Clover dutifully inspected it.

'Wow. That's big. It means…well, I think it means he might be coming to respect you.'

'So long as he respects *you*, I'll be happy.'

'My hero.'

'You'd better believe it, my love.'

'Pity he didn't choose to stay for the reception but he *did* come to the back of beyond to walk his only daughter down the aisle. That's the most attention I've had from him since…well, I can't remember when.'

'I'm happy you're happy.'

'I am.' Clover closed her eyes and once more leaned her cheek against her husband's chest. Content. Relaxed. Loved. She sighed, long and true.

'There's that sigh again,' he remarked.

'It's a sigh of complete and utter happiness be-cause I've found you. I've finally found you. I can live in the town where I belong, practise medicine and start a new chapter in my life with you—my one true love.'

They continued to dance together, not caring whether the music was loud and rocking or slow and sensual. They were lost in their own little world and it was only when the MC said it was time for the traditional garter and bouquet toss that Brandon released his wife with great reluctance.

'To be continued,' he whispered in her ear, and she giggled.

'Promises, promises,' she replied, as they made their way towards the microphone.

'All right, time for all single women to gather in one crazy group, ready for the toss of the bridal bouquet,' Edward Goldmark announced. Clover smiled and took the microphone from Edward, her voice smooth and modulated.

'I caught Ruby's bouquet less than six months ago so perhaps this thing really works!' She laughed, then handed the microphone back to Edward and turned her back to the waiting women.

'On the count of three,' Brandon called, and

together everyone joined in the countdown. On 'three', Clover pitched the bouquet over her head and turned to watch it fall into the waiting arms of Marissa, who had been a widow for over twenty years.

The woman yelped and squealed with delight. 'Yes,' she said with joy. 'Thank you, God. I will be getting married again soon.' And she turned, winking at Greg Filmore. To his credit, the sixty-year-old widower turned beetroot red but smiled at Marissa nonetheless.

'And now for the men,' Edward announced into the microphone, and laughed as Marissa nudged poor Greg into position. Brandon and Clover watched as the men, far more reluctant than the women, made their way into the centre of the dance floor, laughing as Hamilton and Benedict ensured their only single brother Bartholomew was in the mix.

'On three!' Edward said, and again the crowd counted down. Just before Brandon threw the garter, he focused his gaze on Bartholomew as though getting his bearings, then he turned his back to the crowd and threw the garter over head—his plan working to perfection as the garter landed in Bartholomew's half-heartedly open hand.

The crowd cheered, Marissa shrugged but still sidled up close to Greg, while the Goldmark men took great delight in teasing the only bachelor left among them.

'The garter toss doesn't lie,' Hamilton said, pointing to Brandon as though providing proof.

'Finally!' Honeysuckle remarked. 'A good woman is coming your way.'

'But I'm not interested in getting married,' Bartholomew protested, only to be laughed at again by his crazy family.

'Happens to the best of us,' Woody remarked, slapping Bart on the back.

'I wonder who she is?' Ruby asked.

'Whoever she is, she's a lucky woman,' Clover said, gazing into Brandon's eyes. 'To marry a member of the Goldmark family means to be embraced with pure happiness and love.'

'The bride has spoken!' Brandon declared, and everybody cheered!

* * * * *

Mills & Boon® Large Print
Medical

May

June

July

August

THE BROODING DOC'S REDEMPTION	Kate Hardy
AN INESCAPABLE TEMPTATION	Scarlet Wilson
REVEALING THE REAL DR ROBINSON	Dianne Drake
THE REBEL AND MISS JONES	Annie Claydon
THE SON THAT CHANGED HIS LIFE	Jennifer Taylor
SWALLOWBROOK'S WEDDING OF THE YEAR	Abigail Gordon

September

NYC ANGELS: REDEEMING THE PLAYBOY	Carol Marinelli
NYC ANGELS: HEIRESS'S BABY SCANDAL	Janice Lynn
ST PIRAN'S: THE WEDDING!	Alison Roberts
SYDNEY HARBOUR HOSPITAL: EVIE'S BOMBSHELL	Amy Andrews
THE PRINCE WHO CHARMED HER	Fiona McArthur
HIS HIDDEN AMERICAN BEAUTY	Connie Cox

October

NYC ANGELS: UNMASKING DR SERIOUS	Laura Iding
NYC ANGELS: THE WALLFLOWER'S SECRET	Susan Carlisle
CINDERELLA OF HARLEY STREET	Anne Fraser
YOU, ME AND A FAMILY	Sue MacKay
THEIR MOST FORBIDDEN FLING	Melanie Milburne
THE LAST DOCTOR SHE SHOULD EVER DATE	Louisa George